Look for other titles about the WILD AT HEART vet volunteers:

ANIMAL RECORD

Owner's Name Jane Young

Address 1127 Hamilton Street

Animal's Name Yum-Yum

Species Name Canis familiaris

Breed Shih tzu

Age 12 yrs.

Sex Male

Color & Markings Black and White

Weight 11 lbs.

Height ———

TREATMENT

Date

8\1   Bad breath, loss of appetite,
        swollen lymph glands
        Walnut-sized black tumor
        on roof of mouth

Say Good-Bye

Laurie Halse Anderson

American Girl™

Acknowledgments
Thanks to Kimberly Michels, D.V.M.

Published by Pleasant Company Publications
Text Copyright © 2001 by Laurie Halse Anderson
Illustration and Design Copyright © 2001 Pleasant Company

Although Ambler, Pennsylvania, is a real town (a wonderful town!), the setting, characters, and events that take place in this book are all fictional. Any similarity to real persons, living or dead, is coincidental and not intended by the author. This book is not intended as a substitute for your veterinarian. Your vet is the best source of health advice for your pet.

Printed in the United States of America.

01 02 03 04 05 06 07 08 RRD 10 9 8 7 6 5 4 3 2 1

American Girl® and Wild at Heart™ are trademarks of Pleasant Company.

Series Editor: Julie Williams
Art Direction & Design: Joshua Mjaanes
Styling: Jean doPico
Cover and Title Page Photography: Brian Malloy
Newspaper Clipping Photography: Jamie Young

Photo Credits: page 127—Corbis; page 128—Murphy "The Meritorious" Malayter © Steve Milanowski/Meriter Hospital; page 129—The Stock Market Photo Agency, photo by Jon Feingersh; page 130—courtesy of Canine Companions for Independence, Santa Rosa, CA; page 131—© Stephan Simpson 1994, FPG International LLC; page 132—courtesy of Sheila W. Boneham, Perennial Australian Shepherds

A catalog record for this book is available from the Library of Congress

ISBN 1-58485-051-5

Dedication
To Cathy East Dubowski, with friendship and thanks

I'm up early, making French toast—not the Wonder Bread kind, the real stuff, with thick, day-old French bread, fresh strawberries, and powdered sugar on top.

I feel a tug on my shoelaces and look down. "Sneakers . . ." I groan.

My six-month-old pup is having my shoelaces for breakfast. Sneakers is adorable, even though he's a mutt—short-haired, with cute, floppy little triangle ears. He's mostly black with a little bit of brown in spots. He also has white fur around his muzzle, neck, and tummy and four white legs. He looks like he's wearing white kneesocks.

A woman rescued Sneakers and a bunch of other dogs from an awful man who was selling puppies at the farmer's market. The dogs were dirty, starving, and full of worms. Luckily for the pups, the lady brought them in to Wild at Heart Animal Clinic. That's the veterinary clinic that my grandmother, Dr. J.J. MacKenzie, runs out of an office attached to her home.

We found good homes for most of the dogs. But somehow this little mutt won me over—especially since he kept trying to sneak out through the clinic door into Gran's house, like he belonged here. That's how he got the name Sneakers.

But the best part was that Gran decided to let me keep him. My very first pet ever! I guess she figured one stray would cheer up the other.

Right now Sneakers is at my feet playing tug-of-war with my laces. He manages to untie one of my shoes. "Shoo!" I tell him, then laugh at my dumb pun. But Sneakers ignores my command, and I sigh. I love him, but he doesn't mind very well. I guess it's because he's still so young. I'm sure he'll do better when he grows up.

Suddenly I hear someone pounding down the stairs. I roll my eyes. It's my cousin Maggie. She makes more noise than an entire basketball team— of *boys*. She leaps off the second-to-last stair and skids into the kitchen, her reddish hair stuffed up in a baseball cap. She wads her pj's into a ball and crouches down.

"What *are* you doing?" I ask her.

She ignores me. Leaps into the air. Shoots her pj ball into the laundry basket on top of the washer in the corner of the kitchen. "Two points!" she cheers.

Sports. That and animals are the only two things Maggie cares about.

She reaches past me into the upper cabinets and pulls down a box of some kind of candy-flavored, artificially colored cereal. She pours a bowlful, then leaves the opened box on the counter, and grabs the milk jug out of the fridge.

"How can you eat that junk?" I ask her.

She shrugs. "Simple. I spoon it into my mouth, chew, and swallow." She always gobbles things down without taking the time to chew them. She says I'm picky about food. I say she'll eat anything.

Did I mention we're not exactly twins?

"You know what I mean," I tell her. "I'm making French toast. Real French toast. With real French bread. Not those frozen things you like to make in the microwave. Want some?"

"No time." She clunks the bowl down on the table and begins to overfill it with milk. "Basketball camp starts today. My ride will be here any minute."

I shrug and turn back to the stove. "Your loss."

As I flip the first slices of French toast onto a plate, Gran comes in from the clinic.

"Zoe! That smells heavenly!" She unfolds the morning newspaper on the counter and reaches for the coffeepot to refill her cup. "Having a real cook around here certainly makes a difference!"

"Thanks." I grin at the praise and hand her a plate. I don't know what Gran and Maggie did before I moved in. The day I got here, they had absolutely nothing to eat in the house.

I hear Maggie's chair scrape back, hear her plop down in her seat, then—

"Ewww! Gross!"

"Told you," I say. But when I turn around, I realize she's not talking about her cereal. She's talking about something under the table.

I take a quick peek.

Uh-oh. Not again!

Sneakers left a little "present" under the table. And Maggie just put her foot in it.

"Zoh-eee!" Maggie says, drawing out my name in a whine. She pulls off her sneaker and carries it over to the trash can.

"What?"

She cleans off her shoe with a piece of old newspaper. "Did you forget to take Sneakers out *again?*"

Okay, I admit it. The first thing on my mind when I wake up in the morning is not whether the puppy needs to go. I mean, I really do love Sneakers. But I grew up with a live-in housekeeper—and without any pets. I never had to do any chores or think about anybody else when I got up in the morning. So all this is new to me. But I'm trying to do better.

"I was going to," I explain, "as soon as I made breakfast."

Maggie looks at me like I'm a total idiot. "Don't you get it, Zoe? A dog needs to go out first thing—especially a puppy." She goes to the sink and squirts way too much pink antibacterial dishwashing detergent on the sole of her sneaker. She scrubs at it with a paper towel.

Ewww, how can she do that? It's the sink we use when we cook and wash dishes! "Is that sanitary? Shouldn't you do that outside?"

Maggie just rolls her eyes as she washes her hands. After she dries her hands and her shoe, she grabs some cleanser from under the counter and dumps it into the sink. Then she sits back down at the table and digs into her cereal.

Good. Maybe her mouth will be too full of artificial colors and flavors to complain any more about Sneakers and me.

Then she says, "How come you let her get away with this, Gran?"

Wrong. She's not going to let it drop.

"You never let me keep any of the puppies from the clinic," Maggie complains. "But you let her keep Sneakers. You ought to make her look after him."

Gran looks up from her newspaper, her right eyebrow arched. "Maggie," she says firmly, "your cereal's getting soggy."

Maggie gets the message. She shuts up and eats her cereal.

Thanks, Gran, I think—too quickly. Because then she turns that stern look on me. "Zoe, Sneakers is nearly six months old now, but his behavior's not improving."

"It's getting worse," Maggie mumbles into her bowl.

Gran lets that one go. "I realize this is new to you, but Sneakers needs . . ."

She stops and looks around the room. "Where is he, anyway?"

"He's right . . ." I look around. Sneakers has disappeared.

I feel my cheeks flush. I'm too embarrassed to say I don't know where he is. I turn back to the counter so Maggie won't see my face. I pick up the wire whisk and briskly beat the already beaten eggs in the mixing bowl. "Um, he's . . . around."

Maggie snorts.

Gran sighs. "Zoe. You have to be consistent with your puppy training, or he'll never learn."

I stare into the bowl of thick, yellow goo. "I'm sorry, Gran," I say. "I promise I'll do better—"

"Don't promise *Gran*," Maggie says. "Promise poor Sneakers!"

Gran glares at her, and Maggie ducks her head over her bowl.

"It's not fair," I say in my defense. "I try, I really do. But Sneakers just doesn't listen. Couldn't we hire a professional pet walker or something to train him? That's what they have back home."

"Back home" is Manhattan—the heart of New York City—where I was born and raised. You can hire anybody to do anything in the city.

"Up there the streets are filled with dog walkers," I try to explain. "And usually they're walking six or seven dogs at a time."

"Oh, brother," Maggie mumbles.

"It looked pretty efficient to me," I shoot back.

"What's the point of having a dog if you're gonna *pay* somebody else to look after it?" Maggie argues.

I roll my eyes at her. Is she trying to be dense on purpose? "It's just like having a housekeeper to do the dirty work. Then the owners get to spend quality time with their pets. It makes perfect sense to me."

"Ridiculous," Maggie snorts.

"It is not—"

Gran holds up her hands between us like a referee at a boxing match. "All right, girls. This is not a debate here. And this is Zoe's pet, Maggie. You've got your hands full taking care of Sherlock." Sherlock is Maggie's seven-year-old basset hound. He's slow and calm—and trained. What's there to take care of?

I smile smugly. "So," I try again, "can we hire someone?"

"Absolutely not," Gran replies. "You know how I feel about that, Zoe. If you care enough to have a pet, you should care enough to take care of it. Now, I'd appreciate it if you'd clean up this mess, and then—"

"Do I have to?" The whine escapes my lips before I can stop it. I know Gran hates whiners.

"Hey, this is the real world," Maggie says. "We don't have maids here. We clean up our own messes."

"Maggie," Gran warns. "That's enough."

Gran rarely gets really angry at Maggie or me, but she looks as if she's seriously thinking about it this morning as she stares at us both. She opens her mouth to say something, but then we hear the bell over the door to the clinic. Someone's here to see Dr. Mac.

"I have to go," Gran says. "Zoe, please clean up this mess. Then take Sneakers outside."

Maggie grins at me like a Cheshire cat.

"And no more squabbling," she tells us both.

Gran grabs her coffee mug and hurries through the door to the clinic. I stare at her forgotten plate of cold French toast.

Maggie seems to make a point of smacking her lips while she finishes her cereal. I make a point of not noticing.

A horn beeps outside. Maggie turns up her cereal bowl and slurps the last of the milk. The spoon clatters in the bowl as she dumps it in the sink and grabs her backpack.

I glare at the table. A few pink and green O's lie drowned in a puddle of milk.

How can I possibly be related to this girl? She has the table manners of a horse!

"Hey!" I call after her. "What about 'We clean up our own messes here'?"

The slam of the screen door is my only answer.

I grab a rag and wipe up the remains of Maggie's breakfast. Okay, I know it must not be easy for Maggie, the way I moved in on her. Her parents died when she was a baby. So she was raised by Gran and never had to share her or the clinic.

But it's not my fault. It's not like I *asked* to come here. And none of us knew I was going to be here this long.

With a groan, I grab some paper towels and some newspaper from the recycling bin and glare at the mess on the floor. Might as well get this over with. "Sneakers, you little poop factory! Where are you?" I call out.

No answer. I guess he's smart enough to hide out until all this blows over.

I pull out a chair and peer under the table. I hate to seem like such a wimp. Maggie doesn't seem to mind sticking her hands in all kinds of goop—and believe me, we get a lot of icky messes around the clinic with all the sick animals we have.

But I never had to clean up anything before I got here. I mean, my parents got divorced so long ago, my dad's like a character in a movie you barely remember seeing. So it was just me and my mom living in a nice modern apartment building in

Manhattan. Mom was an actress on a daytime soap opera, and she was always at work or rehearsals or auditions. In a lot of ways, she's been more like a big sister to me than a mom. Our housekeeper, Ethel, took care of everything. She got Mom to work on time, washed and ironed all our clothes, and cooked all our meals. She even helped me with my homework and taught me how to French-braid my hair. Ethel kept the place so spotless, I never saw any messes—much less had to clean them up.

I guess I never realized how much work Ethel put into keeping our apartment nice. It was like having an aunt or a fairy godmother living with you. Only she got paid.

Everything was perfect—till Mom's soap got canceled. She was really upset at first, but then she got herself psyched up to move to L.A. to audition for some regular TV series. I was so excited!

Until she told me the rest of the news. She wasn't taking me.

I spray at Sneakers' spot on the floor with disinfectant, then scrub with an old rag. I scrub hard, remembering what Mom said.

She tried to explain that it was for my own good, that she'd be too busy with auditions, casting calls, and getting settled to take me along, and that I'd never get to see her anyway. It wouldn't be fair to me, she said.

But was it fair to leave me behind?

I tried to get her to let me stay in Manhattan with Ethel. I loved Ethel. But Mom said we couldn't afford a housekeeper now that she was out of work. Then Ethel went home to look after her sick brother. And suddenly . . . I didn't have anywhere to go.

At first I dreamed up this fantasy. I would call my long-lost father and go live with him—it would be this wonderful reunion, like straight out of the movies. He'd realize how much he missed me and be thrilled to have me back in his life. Maybe he and Mom would even . . .

"Not an option" was all my mom would say about that.

So Mom came up with an even more bizarre plan. She'd send me to stay with her mom, Dr. J.J. MacKenzie—a person she didn't even get along with all that well herself. Just for a little while, she said. Until the work thing got straightened out.

Once I was here, Gran insisted I enroll in school and finish out the school year. That was in March. Now it's August, and I'm still here.

Sometimes . . . I wonder if my mom's ever going to come get me.

TWO

After I clean up from breakfast, I look for Sneakers, but I can't find him anywhere. Frustrated, I give up and hurry through the door that leads into Gran's clinic.

It's almost hard to remember how strange this place seemed when I first came here. I'd never been around animals much, had never even been to a vet's office before. Wild at Heart was noisier, rowdier, and, well, smellier than I'd ever imagined!

But the biggest surprise was how quickly I fell in love with the animals. Mom's not a pet person, so maybe this new feeling for animals is something I inherited from Gran and just didn't know about till now.

What I've learned about animals is this: They don't care where you're from or what kind of clothes you wear or what your mother does for a living.

They love you for who you are.

That's one reason I'm starting to actually like being here. Not that I'd ever tell Maggie that.

I mean, I still get nervous around some of the animals that show up in Gran's clinic. Especially the weird ones like ferrets and Gila monsters. One guy even brought in a sick tarantula!

I think Mom would be proud of me if she could see what I do here. I work as a vet volunteer along with several other kids: Brenna Lake, Sunita Patel, David Hutchinson, and Maggie, of course. They started working together when the clinic was full of sick puppies—including Sneakers—and Gran was desperate for help. The puppies had all been bought from a man at the farmer's market who was running a puppy mill—an illegal business where dogs are bred in really rotten conditions, just so somebody can make a fast buck. I arrived in the middle of it all and had to jump right in. We all did such a good job, Gran said, that she decided to keep us on as volunteers.

We get along pretty well, even though we're all different. Now that it's summer vacation, most of us help out every day.

This morning the others are already here, ready to go to work.

"Good morning!" Gran says with a big smile as she comes out of her office. "I'm *so* glad you're here today."

"Do you have a lot of patients today, Dr. Mac?" Sunita asks. "Any cats?" Sunita loves cats.

"I've got something better," Gran says, grinning. She holds up a clipboard with a list. "A lot of chores."

Everyone groans.

Gran reads down the list. "The supply closet needs to be replenished. Sunita, can you take care of that? And the kennels need some cleaning— we're expecting a lot of boarders this weekend . . ."

There's a lot of good-natured complaining as she goes down her list, but nobody really means it. We all feel pretty lucky to get to volunteer at a cool place like Wild at Heart.

The bell over the door rings again. I look up and see my favorite client.

"Yum-Yum!" I exclaim. I run over and scoop the cute black-and-white dog into my arms. "What are you doing here, you little sweetie pie?" I say, stroking his long, silky hair. "Are you sick?"

"It's an emergency!" jokes his owner, Jane Young. "He's having a bad-hair day—and he's got a big date!"

I laugh, and Yum-Yum licks my face. Yum-Yum is a tiny dog called a shih tzu. He's not a puppy—this is as big as he'll ever get. He almost looks like an expensive stuffed animal. Jane is an old friend of Gran's. She owns a beauty salon, so she *would* have a dog with long, brushable hair! Gran's been letting me take care of Yum-Yum's grooming this summer.

"We just got a last-minute call to visit the kids' cancer ward at the hospital," Jane explains. "You know, just to cheer them up a little. The dog that usually goes in on Monday can't make it today, so I agreed to fill in. Can you do him right now?"

"Sure, we've got time," says Gran.

I take Yum-Yum and Jane back into the grooming area and slip on an apron. Washing a dog can get really messy—especially if the dog isn't too happy about having a bath! Yum-Yum doesn't fuss at all, though, even when I dab a small amount of ointment into his eyes to protect them from the shampoo.

Next I put cotton balls in his ears to keep the water out. I laugh. On Yum-Yum, they look like tiny little earmuffs!

Talking softly to Yum-Yum, I turn on the sprayer and check to make sure the water is warm, but not too warm. Then I hold the sprayer about an inch from his back and soak his coat down to the skin.

Gran taught me an important lesson about bathing animals: Be careful never to spray them in the face. It really upsets them.

Once Yum-Yum is good and wet, I soap him up with a mild doggie shampoo. When I shampooed Yum-Yum the very first time, I wanted to use my salon shampoo and conditioner that I brought from New York. Mom always said it was the best brand for shiny, silky hair. I thought it would make Yum-Yum smell great and make him look like a doggie movie star. But Gran told me that you should never use people shampoo on dogs. It can be too harsh.

Yum-Yum's tail wags as I gently rub the soap through his coat. Some animals hate to be groomed, but Yum-Yum seems to enjoy his shampoo. He doesn't try to squirm away. And he looks like he's smiling!

When I'm finished, I rub him down with a towel, then use a blow-dryer set on a quiet, low-temperature setting to dry him.

"If you ever get tired of the animal business, you've got a job at my salon," Jane jokes.

"This is a lot more fun than some of the things we have to do here," I tell her as I comb Yum-Yum's soft hair. *Like clean up dog poop!*

Gran stops by in between patients. "Yum-Yum!

What a handsome pup you are." She smiles at me. "How's our groomer doing?"

"Great," Jane tells her. "Yum-Yum's always glad to see Zoe." Then she turns back to me. "Say, how would you like to come with me today and see Yum-Yum do his stuff?"

"You mean to the hospital?"

Jane nods. "What do you say, J.J.?" she asks Gran. "Can you spare your assistant for an hour or so?"

"Can I, Gran?" I ask hopefully. "Please?"

"Sure," Gran says. "Things are kind of slow around here today. And don't worry, we'll save some cleanup for you to do when you get back." I know she's teasing a little, though she barely cracks a smile. And I also know there really will be chores for me to do when I get back!

"Thanks, Gran!"

I hear a little bark and look down at my feet.

Sneakers has snuck into the clinic again.

"I've got one more thing to do before I go, though," I tell Jane. She looks down and laughs. Gran shakes her head.

Sneakers has peed on the floor!

THREE

I hold Yum-Yum in my lap as Jane drives us to the hospital. It's a beautiful, hot August day, so we roll the windows down and drive with the wind in our hair.

When we pull into the parking lot, I stare up at the huge hospital building. So many windows . . . I think about all the people inside and why they're there.

Suddenly I feel really weird.

When I lived in Manhattan with my mom, I got to go lots of places with her. I've traveled to other countries. Been to fancy restaurants, the theater, and the ballet. Mom would even take me to the set of her soap. She liked to brag that for a kid my age, I could talk to just about anyone, even grown-ups.

But I've never been in the hospital. Never even visited anybody—especially sick kids.

I try to ignore the strange feeling in the pit of my stomach. I put on a smile and walk through the automatic doors into the main lobby. Everything looks cheerful, but in a forced kind of way. Like we're all trying hard to pretend that nobody's sick, as if nothing's wrong.

Jane leads me down a long hallway. The children's cancer ward is on the first floor, through some swinging doors.

It looks just like the hospital from the soap my mom was on, except the doctors and nurses don't all look like gorgeous models and movie stars. They look pretty nice, though.

The place smells like disinfectant. Colored drawings dot the faded green walls like wildflowers. Pictures of rainbows, of mommies and daddies. Signs that say "I love you, Dr. Bill!"

As Jane checks in at the nurses' desk, I peek down the hall and into the nearest room.

Oh, my gosh! There's a girl about my age propped up in bed watching cartoons—and she's totally bald!

I've heard that chemotherapy—the drugs they give people to try to cure cancer—can make people lose their hair. But I've never actually seen anybody it's happened to.

I suddenly feel very conspicuous with my thick blond hair streaming down below my shoulders. I wish I'd skipped the shampoo and blow-dry this morning—wish I'd simply stuffed my hair up under a baseball cap like Maggie.

I'm speechless.

I mean, it's one thing to be able to ask a smiling soap star for an autograph or to order from a waiter using the French that you've learned at school.

But what do you say to a girl without any hair?

I hug Yum-Yum to my chest. I'm really not prepared for this.

Then I feel an arm slip around my shoulders. "Don't worry, Zoe," Jane says softly, with a reassuring smile. "They're normal kids like you. They've just had some really rotten luck."

"Yeah," I whisper.

"Cancer's a stinking disease," she adds, "but you can't catch it from another person. And it doesn't change these kids in here." She taps her chest over her heart.

"But their hair . . ."

Jane chuckles softly. "That's how I got into this in the first place," she explains. "I do free hairstyling for chemotherapy patients. And if they want, I help them with wigs till their own hair grows back in.

But wigs are uncomfortable for a lot of kids. So they feel better going *au naturel."* She winks at me. "You'll get used to it."

I smile. But inside I'm thinking, *How could you ever get used to it?*

Suddenly Yum-Yum spots a tall skinny kid at the end of the hall. I bite my lip.

Bald head. Shapeless hospital gown. Oh, gosh! At this distance, I can't even tell if it's a boy or a girl!

Yum-Yum barks and wriggles in my arms.

"Go ahead," Jane says. "You can just put him down and let him go."

I stoop down and release him.

The kid grins and throws a small red ball. As Yum-Yum dashes after it down the hall, I hear kids squeal and call out his name as they wander out of their rooms. Normal kid sounds. Not what you'd expect in a hospital.

Yum-Yum catches the ball and carries it over to another patient—a young girl who looks about eight.

"Give!" the young girl commands.

Instantly Yum-Yum lays the ball at her feet.

"Good dog!" the girl praises him. She gives his head a good scratching.

"I wish Sneakers would behave like that," I tell Jane. "I mean, don't get me wrong, he's a wonderful

dog, and he's always there for me when I'm sad."
The way Mom used to be. "But he sure doesn't mind me very well."

"Don't worry," Jane says. "He'll learn. He's still a puppy. Just give it time, and stick with it. Then maybe one day, you can train Sneakers to do therapy visits, too."

I roll my eyes. "No way. He's barely housebroken."

"Well, you do have to get that down first!" she chuckles.

I follow Jane down to a lounge area. The windows look out onto a pretty garden in front of the hospital. There are lots of plants around the room, plus several jigsaw puzzles and a chess set laid out on some tables.

Many of the kids gather around. They're all different ages, from teenagers to really little kids. Some have hair, some don't. Some look okay. Others look really sick—pale and thin and tired, like they've had the flu or something.

But they all smile at the sight of Yum-Yum.

"Hey, Michael, check it out. That dog looks like a runaway wig!" a teenage boy jokes. I guess he hasn't seen Yum-Yum here before.

"Huh? Don't make fun of my main man!" the boy named Michael replies. "Just wait till you see him do his tricks!" He whistles softly and claps his hands. "Yum-Yum! Come here, boy."

Yum-Yum trots over.

"Sit," Michael says, and Yum-Yum instantly obeys. Michael grabs a doggie treat from a jar and holds it in the air. "Sit up, Yum-Yum."

I'm amazed when Yum-Yum stands up on his two hind feet. Michael even gets him to walk a few steps. The kids laugh and clap. So do I.

"Make him roll over!" a girl about my age shouts.

Michael makes a rolling motion with his right hand. "Roll over, Yum-Yum. Roll over."

Yum-Yum rolls over and over on the linoleum floor.

The kids clap and cheer as if they were at the circus.

"Now watch this," Michael tells the other boy. "Take a bow, Yum-Yum."

Michael dips his head.

Yum-Yum sticks out one little paw and bends low over it. He really looks like he's bowing!

"Michael Maltin," a nurse calls out.

The laughter dies as quickly as if someone had turned off a TV. For a moment, Michael looks tired and much older. "More blood work for Nurse

Bennett," he complains to his buddy. "Yuck." Then he turns back to Yum-Yum. "See you later, pal."

Yum-Yum barks, and Michael laughs. "Okay, little buddy. Shake!" He sticks out his hand, and Yum-Yum puts his small paw into it. Michael gives the paw a gentle shake.

When Michael turns back to the nurse, he looks like himself again. "Okay, Dracula," he tells her dramatically, holding out his arms in a gesture of mock helplessness. "Do your worst!"

Nurse Bennett just laughs, shakes her head, and leads Michael down the hall.

As the kids line up to shake Yum-Yum's paw, I turn to Jane. "I can't believe it. Yum-Yum ought to be on TV! How did you teach him all those things?"

Jane chuckles. "When he was little, I used to hold up treats for him. That's how he learned to stand on his hind legs. Some of the tricks are things the kids here at the hospital have taught him. But remember, Yum-Yum's nearly thirteen! So he's had years of practice."

A little girl who looks about six or seven comes up to us.

"Hi, Stephanie," Jane says. "What's new?"

"My mom brought me some new butterfly clips." She holds them up proudly for us to see.

"Oh, they're gorgeous!" Jane coos.

I'm speechless. Her mother brought her hair clips? What kind of mom would do something like that? Poor Stephanie doesn't have any hair!

Stephanie nods. "Mommy says they're for when my hair grows back in. She says that'll be really soon. And she says it will be prettier than ever!"

I nearly blush, I feel so dumb. What kind of mom would do that? A smart one. She's giving Stephanie something to look forward to.

Just then Yum-Yum scampers up to Stephanie and licks her leg.

Stephanie squeals with laughter. "Hello, Yum-Yum." She bends down and gives the little dog a kiss on top of his head. "I don't have any hair right now," she tells him. "So you can borrow these if you want." She looks up at Jane. "Is it okay?" she asks.

"Okay with me," Jane says. "As long as Yum-Yum doesn't mind."

Stephanie plops down on the floor beside Yum-Yum and goes to work. She puts the butterfly clips in the long, silky hair around his ears.

"Gorgeous!" Stephanie pronounces.

I'm amazed that Yum-Yum doesn't mind. He's so good with kids.

Stephanie gives him a hug, then she makes a

disgusted face. "Yum-Yum, I love you—but you need to brush your teeth!"

Some of the other kids laugh, but I notice that Jane is frowning.

"Maybe it's that new dog food I've been buying," she says to a nurse. "I think it's giving him bad breath."

"Check the ingredients for garlic," the nurse jokes. "That's what always does it for me."

Suddenly Yum-Yum breaks away from the crowd of kids and takes off for a corner of the room.

A girl is sitting there in a wheelchair with her back to the others. A teddy-bear balloon tied to one handle bobs for attention, but the girl doesn't seem to know it's there. She's got a large blue bucket hat tugged down low over her brow, shielding her eyes as she stares out the window at nothing. Her thin hands lie forgotten in her lap.

Yum-Yum sits up by her slippered feet and barks at the girl. She doesn't move. It's like she doesn't even hear him.

"What's wrong with that girl?" I quietly ask Jane.

Jane sighs. "That's Emma Morgan. Poor kid. They tell me she's having a hard time of it. We all try to get her to socialize with the other kids, but she just doesn't seem interested." Jane smiles wistfully.

"Most kids are just naturally hopeful, so even when they get sick with cancer, they roll with the punches pretty well, especially if they have good support. But Emma—she seems awfully down. Never talks much. Even Michael can't get her to laugh."

"That *is* serious," I say. I watch her for a moment. "She seems lonesome."

"That could account for a lot of it," Jane says. "Apparently her parents are divorced, her mom works full-time, and her brother's away at college in California, so she's here by herself for most of the time." Jane lowers her voice. "I don't think she hears from her dad much."

That's something I can definitely relate to.

"Nurse Bennett told me a neighbor had to bring her in for treatment this time," she adds.

As I go over to get Yum-Yum, I see the girl's face reflected in the glass window. She's looking at me—at my hair. Her brown eyes are large, beautiful . . . and hopeless.

Just like some of the hurt and scared animals I've seen come into the clinic.

I'm learning how to deal with animals like that, but I'm not sure what to do with people.

I put on my best smile, scoop up Yum-Yum, and walk around so Emma can see me. "Hi, I'm Zoe," I say. "How're you doing?"

My words seem to hang in the air.

What a dumb thing to say! Of course she's doing terribly—she's got cancer! I try to cover up my goof by laying Yum-Yum in her lap.

"Doesn't Yum-Yum look cute?" I say. "I just washed and blow-dried his hair . . . this morning."

Cringe! What's wrong with me? Hair, hair, hair. It's like when they say don't think about pink elephants—then it's all you can think about!

It's not like me to say the wrong thing. It must be nerves.

But Emma doesn't seem to notice my dumb remarks. Slowly, shyly, she reaches out to stroke Yum-Yum's soft fur. And when Yum-Yum barks and wags his little tail, Emma actually smiles.

It's like the sun coming out on a cloudy day.

I can see why, in spite of the sadness, Jane likes to come here.

Maybe now I can get Emma to talk a little. I don't know what it's like to have cancer, but I do know what it's like to feel lonely and miss your mom. And to have a dad who's totally out of the picture.

I notice a book tucked down beside her thin legs. "So, I see you've got a book there," I begin awkwardly. "I like to read, too. What are you reading?"

"Um . . ." Emma looks at the book as if it appeared there by magic. She picks it up, then shrugs and holds it out to me.

I don't recognize the title, so I open the book. On the title page, someone has quickly scrawled, "To Emma, from Dad." I flip through the pages and frown. It's a story about talking bunnies! I can tell by the big type that the book is for a very young reader. But Emma is at least my age. I guess "Dad" doesn't come around very often if he thinks his twelve-year-old daughter is still reading books like this.

"Oh, this looks interesting," I fib, trying to be polite.

Emma shoots me a look that says *Liar!* Like she's developed radar lately for people who don't tell her the truth.

So I lean forward and look her straight in the eye. "For a first-grader," I say in a goofy voice.

Then something happens—something that feels like a miracle.

Emma actually laughs out loud.

I laugh, too, and Yum-Yum barks, happily wagging his fanlike tail.

"Dads," she says, rolling her eyes. "What are you going to do?"

"Tell me about it," I agree.

I reach for a chair to drag closer so that I can sit down. Maybe now I can get Emma to talk some.

But then Nurse Bennett calls me. "Sorry, Zoe. It's time to go."

Darn! Just when I was getting somewhere! I gently scoop up Yum-Yum from Emma's lap. "It was nice meeting you," I say. "We'll see you again soon."

But the sun has already gone back behind the clouds.

"Yeah," Emma says vaguely. She's facing the window again, staring out at nothing.

As I carry Yum-Yum down the hall, a lot of the kids walk along with us, petting Yum-Yum and telling us good-bye. Yum-Yum barks happily. I feel as if I was just getting comfortable.

I'm quiet as we head down the hall toward the lobby.

"You were great," Jane tells me. "I know it's not easy the first time. But they're terrific kids. And a lot of them aren't just sick. They're also far away from home, away from their family and friends. It really gives them a lift to have folks—and dogs!— visit them."

"Kind of makes you appreciate . . ." But I can't

finish the sentence. I've got a funny little lump in my throat.

When we step out of the hospital, the sun seems to be shining brighter. Or maybe I'm just looking at everything a little bit differently.

I put Yum-Yum down on the sidewalk. He trots along a few steps ahead of us as we walk toward the car.

I watch him, amazed. He's so well trained, Jane doesn't even have to use a leash with him. He always stays by her side.

Jane and I are mostly silent on our way to the car. Sometimes that makes me feel nervous around grown-ups, like I need to be thinking up something interesting to say. But it feels okay with Jane. I'm glad she doesn't try to make small talk.

When we reach the car, I pick up Yum-Yum and get into the passenger side of the front seat. He sits nicely at my feet as I buckle my seat belt. Then I scoop him up into my lap. He sits up tall and looks like he's smiling. Panting, he peeks out the side window, as if he's excited about driving and wants to see where we're going next. Gran says some dogs hate riding in cars, sometimes because their owners only drive them in cars when they're taking them to have something painful done at the vet's office. I can tell Jane takes Yum-Yum with her in the car a lot.

I smile down at the pooch as we drive away. Then I notice something—something around Yum-Yum's mouth. "Do you have a tissue, Jane? I think one of the kids must have slipped Yum-Yum a messy treat."

"Sure." Keeping her eyes on the road, she reaches for her purse on the seat between us and unzips a pocket. "Look in here and see if you see some."

I pull a tissue out of one of those tiny purse packs, then use it to wipe gently around Yum-Yum's mouth. "There you go, sweetie. You're nice and—" I stop when I look at the tissue. It has a small streak of something red on it. And it doesn't look like food—it looks like blood. Is Yum-Yum hurt?

When we stop at a red light, I lay my hand on Jane's arm. "Jane, look."

"What?" She frowns, puzzled by the tissue I'm holding up.

"Do you think Yum-Yum hurt his mouth chasing that ball?" I ask.

"Maybe . . ." She lifts Yum-Yum's chin with her finger. "Look here, little guy," she says, playfully stern. "What have you done to yourself?" She peers closely at him.

Someone behind us beeps. The light has turned green. Jane turns back to the road. A light frown creases her brow as she drives through the intersection. "I'm sure it's nothing."

"Yeah," I say, feeling a little nervous. I crumple the tissue and throw it away in the tiny trash bag Jane keeps on the floor.

"Yum-Yum's due for a checkup anyway," Jane goes on. "When we get back to the clinic, I'll see if the doc can take a look at the old boy."

FOUR

As soon as we get back to the clinic, Jane and Yum-Yum wait for Gran while I take Sneakers outside. But he won't, you know, do his business.

"Go ahead, Sneakers. Be a good boy." My voice drops to a whisper. "Come on. Just do it . . . Please?"

I stand over him, my fists on my hips. "What are you waiting for?" I hate to rush the poor dog, but I'm in a hurry. I want to go find out about Yum-Yum. I want to make sure he's all right. How long should it take to go to the bathroom? "Come on, Sneakers. Go! I don't have all day."

David comes out of the clinic and stops to watch me. Nothing like having an audience. "Hey, how's it going?" he asks.

"It's not," I say grumpily.

David laughs and shakes his long bangs out of his eyes. "What's wrong?"

I feel kind of embarrassed talking about this with a boy. But Gran always says there's no need to be squeamish about the bodily functions of animals. "I . . . I'm having trouble training him," I finally say. "You know, to go outside. Do you have any ideas?"

David chuckles. "Not me. All I know about is training horses. And housebreaking is one thing you don't have to worry about with them!" David is totally crazy about horses. Whenever Gran has to make a visit to a stable to treat a sick horse, David's the first to volunteer.

Sneakers barks happily. He runs a circle around me, then flops down on the ground. He sniffs something in the grass and starts to paw at it.

This is so embarrassing! How are you supposed to *make* a dog go to the bathroom anyway? I'm totally clueless.

"Maybe you should take him behind some bushes or something," David jokes. "Maybe he's too embarrassed to go in front of you."

"Thanks a lot, David."

"No problem!" He laughs and heads across the street, toward his house.

"How come you're leaving?" I call after him. I know David loves this place. He says he's been pestering Gran for years to let him volunteer.

"I've got to go baby-sit my little sister Ashley because my big brother Brian has more important things to do," he says with a scowl. "Can you believe it? Instead of staying here and saving lives all afternoon, I'll be playing Let's Go to the Mall. There ought to be a law against forcing boys to play Barbies with five-year-old girls!"

I laugh, and for once I think that maybe it's better to be an only child than the middle of three.

"Hey, about Sneakers," he calls back over his shoulder. "Maybe you should ask Maggie. She knows a lot about dogs."

I frown at David's back as he hurries across the street to his house. Go ask Maggie? *Hmph!* The last thing I want to do is admit to her what a failure I am at training Sneakers. Maybe I should check Gran's library for a book . . .

I look toward the clinic. I love Sneakers and want to do a good job with him, but I'm dying to go inside to see what's up with Yum-Yum. "Okay, Sneakers," I say, trying to sound firm. "A couple more minutes. Tops. Then I'm taking you back in."

I tap my foot on the ground and glare at him. Nothing.

"Come on, Sneak. I have to check on Yum-Yum!"
Maybe he *is* nervous with me watching. I turn

around and pretend to ignore him for a minute, then I turn back around.

Still nothing.

I give up. Maybe he just doesn't have to go. I take him back inside the house. I check to see that he has fresh water and give him a little doggie treat. "Now, be a good dog," I say. He looks up at me with his adorable brown eyes, and all my crabbiness melts away. I bend down and give him a hug. "Don't worry," I say softly. "We're *both* new at this! We'll get better soon, I promise!"

Then I hurry over to the clinic. I find Gran and Jane in the Dolittle Room with Yum-Yum. Both of Gran's examining rooms are named after famous animal doctors from books: Dr. Dolittle from the book by Hugh Lofting, and Herriot from James Herriot, the pen name of an English veterinarian who wrote fiction based on his experiences. I just read one of his most famous books, *All Creatures Great and Small*.

"Can I come in?" I ask.

Gran looks up at her friend. "Okay, Jane?"

Jane smiles. "Sure, come on in, Zoe. Yum-Yum's always glad to have you around."

Yum-Yum wags his tail when he sees me, and I smile at him, but I stay back so I won't get in Gran's way. Yum-Yum looks so tiny on Gran's big examining table.

First she checks Yum-Yum's heart and lungs with a stethoscope. Then she moves her strong, gentle hands over the little dog's body, feeling here and there.

Yum-Yum pants happily and wags his tail. He thinks Dr. Mac is petting him, but I know Gran is giving him a thorough examination.

Next Gran shines a little light into Yum-Yum's eyes. Then she gently opens his mouth and shines a light inside. Yum-Yum's mouth is so tiny, I'm surprised she can see anything.

Gran's brows knit as she feels Yum-Yum's teeth—like she's checking for a loose tooth. Do dogs this age still lose teeth?

Then she shines her light all around the inside of Yum-Yum's mouth. She pauses when she looks at the roof of his mouth, like she's trying to see something more clearly.

"Have you noticed anything unusual in his behavior lately?" she asks Jane.

Jane shakes her head. "No. I mean, I don't think so. Not really . . ."

Gran keeps looking at the roof of Yum-Yum's mouth. You might not notice if you hadn't been around Gran much, but I see something change in her expression.

Jane notices, too. She frowns and starts to fiddle with her hands. "Well, I have noticed Yum-Yum's not eating quite as much as he usually does. And he's started taking more naps. But I guess I just thought it was this summer heat—and his age. Kind of like me!" She's trying to joke, but I can tell she's suddenly worried. She bites her lip. "Nothing to be concerned about, is it, J.J.?"

I look at Gran, expecting her to say, "No, just a routine question." But she doesn't say that. She lets go of Yum-Yum's mouth and moves on to his ears. She just keeps looking, checking, and I know something's up, even though her face is calm as she continues to feel Yum-Yum with experienced hands. It's almost as if her fingers have sight, looking for things beneath the surface. "How many of these therapy visits has he been doing?"

"A lot," Jane admits. "Maybe too many. It's just, there's a lot of demand for therapy dogs. More than we can handle. The kids are so crazy about Yum-Yum that I hate to say no."

Gran nods. She is gently feeling along Yum-Yum's neck, checking his lymph glands.

"Um, also . . ." Jane looks nervous, but she tries

to chuckle. "I've noticed he's had pretty bad breath lately, even though I brush his teeth and have them cleaned regularly. Is that old age, too?"

Gran smirks. "Maybe a little."

Jane and I watch silently as Gran's hands go over Yum-Yum's neck and ears again. I study her face closely. It stays calm and cool, yet friendly—but then . . . there's a tiny change in her expression again. Like she's noticed something. *What?*

I bite my thumbnail and wait.

"J.J.," Jane says, forcing a bright laugh, "say something. You're making me nervous."

Gran seems to have finished her examination. She rubs her forehead a moment, sighs, and runs a hand through her short white hair. When she looks up, I see it in her eyes. Something's wrong.

"Jane, I've found a few things," she says simply.

Things? What does that mean?

"What kind of things?" Jane asks anxiously.

Gran smiles kindly at her as she gives Yum-Yum's head a good rub. "Yum-Yum's lymph glands are swollen. And I've found a black tumor on the roof of Yum-Yum's mouth—"

"A tumor!" Jane exclaims. "You mean . . ."

Gran lays a calming hand on her friend's arm. "I think we should keep Yum-Yum here overnight and do a few tests. I'd like to take some chest X rays and do a biopsy."

"A biopsy!" I gasp.

Mom's character on the soap had to get a biopsy once. That's how I know what it is. It's what they do to find out if a lump is cancerous.

"You mean . . . like in cancer?" I ask.

Tears well up in Jane's eyes. "Oh, my gosh! He's going to be all right, though, isn't he, J.J.? *Isn't* he?"

I can see Gran cringe a little as she hands Jane a tissue. "It might be nothing," she says, nodding. "But I need to do some tests to make a diagnosis."

"Sure, J.J." Jane's voice softens, and she seems to go limp. It's so strange. Jane is always so bubbly and cheerful—Gran says she was probably born smiling. So it's even weirder to see her face now. I can tell—she knows something's wrong, too.

"What exactly do you have to do to him?" Jane asks hesitantly.

"I'll put him to sleep for fifteen minutes," Gran says. "And I'll make a very small incision in the tumor in his mouth so that I can remove a tiny amount of skin tissue. Then I'll look at it under a microscope."

"And?" Jane asks.

"Any black pigment in the cells would indicate

a malignancy."

"Cancer," Jane says. She picks up Yum-Yum and buries her face in the small dog's fur.

After a moment, she tells Yum-Yum, "You know, sweetie, I've got to get back to the shop, and I'm going to be so busy. Dr. Mac says you can stay here tonight. Won't that be fun? What do you say? Want to have a sleepover with Dr. Mac and Zoe?"

Yum-Yum barks and wags his tail, and I smile in spite of my worried feelings.

"You'll take good care of him?" she asks.

"Of course," Gran says. "And I'm sure Zoe wouldn't mind looking after him, would you?"

"I'd be glad to." I flash Jane one of my brightest smiles, hoping I've inherited some of Mom's acting genes, because right now I feel like bursting into tears. *Cancer!* Yum-Yum? It can't be true!

Jane writes down a lot of instructions for me. What to feed Yum-Yum. When to feed him. What his favorite TV show is. A lot of little things. It seems to make her feel better.

Then she gives Yum-Yum a kiss on the top of his head. "You be a good boy, and I'll see you soon," she says. She wipes her eyes with the tissue and hurries out.

I wait for Jane to leave. Then I whirl around to

face Gran and blurt out, "Does he *really* have cancer? I didn't know dogs could get that."

Gran nods. "A lot of dogs get cancer, just like people do. Especially as they get older. But come on, now. Yum-Yum's a tough little dog. So let's think positive. Maybe it's nothing. Nothing at all."

Gran is trying to make me feel better, but she can't fool me. I can tell Gran is worried. And so am I.

FIVE

Hi, honey! Did you get my message?"

It's my mom on the phone, calling from California. I'm sitting at the receptionist's desk in the clinic, sorting through a pile of files.

"No!" I exclaim. "When did you call? Are you coming to get me?"

Silence on the other end of the phone.

"Uh, well—" Mom's enthusiasm fades a little. "Not exactly, sweetie. What I meant was, I've been working on my ability to communicate with people mentally—ESP, telepathy, that kind of stuff. I thought it might help me get some work." She laughs at her joke. "So I tried sending you a mental message."

"I guess my line was busy."

Mom laughs. "Zoe! That's very funny!"

"So . . . what was your message?" I ask.

"I think I've got a part in a sitcom!" she almost squeals.

"What? I thought you already had a part."

"Oh, didn't Gran tell you?" she asks. "That show is on hold. I don't know if it will ever go back into production. And it really wasn't a very good part anyway. But this one—it's a real winner!"

"That's great!" I say. My hopes swell like a birthday balloon.

"Well, it's not for sure or anything," Mom goes on, "but it looks really good—"

"Oh, Mom! Tell me all about it!"

"Well, it's a callback for a pilot," she begins.

A little air seeps out of my balloon. "A callback?"

"Yeah. I went to an audition, and now they're calling me back for a second read. That means they're seriously considering me for the role!"

"Oh."

I guess I sound disappointed, because Mom insists, "No, Zoe, that's really good! That means I've almost got the part." She takes a deep breath. "Oh, Zoe, doll, this part was made for me—it *is* me!"

"That's great, Mom. So now what happens?"

"I'll read again tomorrow, and then I should hear something next week, maybe. But I gotta tell you, sweetheart, it's looking like a sure thing."

"Great!" I say. Then I try to send her a psychic message of my own.

She doesn't get it.

So I try the direct route. "So when can I come . . ." I start to say "home," but "home" to me is New York. I've never even been to California. So I just say ". . . out there?"

Again, silence on the other end. Not good.

"Mom?"

"Soon, honey. I promise."

Soon. One of the vaguest words in the English language. *Soon* can mean anything. Seconds, minutes, days . . . years!

"How soon is soon?" I ask in a small voice.

"Well, you see, like I said, the part is for a pilot," she explains. "For a midseason replacement."

This "sure thing" is sounding more unsure every second.

"So if I get the part—" She laughs. "I mean, *when* I get the part, we'll shoot a pilot episode. Then they'll use that to try to sell the series. And if one of the major networks picks it up, we'll go into full production and be on the air by January."

She goes on and on in this really excited voice about how her agent says it's her lucky break, that this is how a lot of actresses break into the big time.

She sounds more like a hyper little girl than a mom.

"So . . ." I persist. "When do you *think* I can come out there? I mean, it's not all that long till school starts again, Mom, you know? And I don't want to start here if I'm going to move to California soon—"

"Zoe. Honey . . ."

I stop, and a lump fills my throat.

Especially when Mom says, "You might have to go ahead and start school there—"

"Mom!"

"I know, honey," she says. "I know how you're feeling. Believe me, I'm not happy about this, either."

Could have fooled me.

"Everything's so . . . you know, up in the air," she goes on, "but if this all works out . . . well, Zoe, sweetheart, this could really be my big break. The one I've been waiting for."

I don't say anything. For a moment, I don't trust myself to speak without crying. I stare down at the files on the desk. The name Yum-Yum swims in front of my eyes. I trace Gran's bold, scrawling cursive with my fingertip as I blink back tears.

"This will be good for us, Zoe," Mom insists. "You'll see."

When I still don't say anything, she sighs. "Zoe, honey . . ." Her voice is soft, pleading. "Aren't you happy for me?"

I try to swallow the lump. "Sure, Mom," I manage to say, forcing a smile into my voice. And I *am* happy for her. I'm just not happy for me. "So . . ." I force myself to joke, "Am I first in line for an autograph?"

Mom laughs—a laugh that belongs on TV. Warm, golden, full of music. "You betcha, doll! And just wait, Zoe. This is going to be great for us. I promise. Just you wait."

Wait, she says. What choice do I have?

"So," I start again. "Are you at least going to get to come visit soon?" Surely she has time for that.

"Zoe, honey . . ."

I wish she'd stop saying that! "Too busy, huh?" I say before she can.

"You know I want to, doll. And I will—soon. I promise. It's just that, I mean, if this thing goes through, I'm going to be really busy till we get the pilot shot—"

"I understand, Mom. Really," I say.

"Oh, Zoe, you're the best," Mom gushes. "I'll send you some autographs of the other actors. For your collection. How's that sound?"

"Great," I say.

"So listen, I've gotta go. Is Gran there? I guess I ought to speak to her a sec."

"Sure, Mom. I'll get her."

"Bye, sweetheart! Love ya!"

"Yeah," I choke out. "Love ya, too."

I lay down the phone and stare at the receiver. I want to pick it up again. Talk to her about Yum-Yum. Tell her how scared I am that he might have cancer. I want to tell her about the kids I saw at the hospital, the ones with no hair. How sad it made me feel. And how Sneakers is determined to drive me crazy.

I want to tell her . . . that I really, really miss her.

But she's so happy about her audition. What good would it do to make her feel bad? I don't want her to come get me because she feels guilty. I want her to come get me because she misses me too much to go another day without me.

Tell her, I think. *Tell her you miss her so badly it hurts. Beg her to come get you.*

But it's easier not to ask. Easier not to hear her say she can't.

Instead, I buzz Gran on the intercom.

As Gran picks up the phone, I hang around, pretending to sort and stack files. But it's really so I can eavesdrop on their conversation. I can hear

Gran's strong, clear voice through the open examining-room door.

"Rose!" I hear Gran say cheerfully. "How are things going?"

Gran does a lot of nodding, but her smile is fading away. "But, Rose, you really need to . . . "

I try to get closer so I can hear what my mom needs to do. I carry a stack of folders over to a filing cabinet. But Sneakers chooses that moment to run into the clinic. When he strikes a familiar pose, I plop the files back on the desk and reach for him. "Oh, no, you don't!" I scoop him up and dash outdoors in the nick of time. For once he makes a puddle outside, not on the kitchen floor. I guess that counts as a success.

I sit down on the steps leading to the deck and clap my hands for Sneakers to come. He runs over and licks my outstretched hand. Then my arm. Then my face! "Oh, Sneakers! What would I do without you!" I say as I scoop him into my lap. But that makes me think about Jane and how one day soon, she may have to do without Yum-Yum.

I hug Sneakers tightly, and he squirms a little, but I don't want to let go. "Do you think Yum-Yum's going to be all right?" I whisper into his ear.

Sneakers yaps happily, and I decide to take that as a good sign. But I won't stop worrying until Gran tells me everything's okay.

Just then Brenna comes out of Wild at Heart, walking a freshly groomed poodle. I have to laugh.

"What's so funny?" Brenna asks.

"You, that's what," I reply, pointing. "A poodle? Not exactly your style."

Brenna shrugs and grins. She's wearing boots, and clothes that look as if they were dug out of her brother's laundry hamper. Her long brown hair is pulled back into a quick braid. She'd be really pretty if she'd just let me dress her and do something with her hair.

But Brenna's not a fancy kind of girl. And she's definitely not into fancy, poodly pets. Her favorite animals are anything wild. Her parents are "wildlife rehabilitators." They rescue injured or sick animals, then take care of them until they're well enough to be released back into the wild. And her pet? Poe—a pet crow!

"I want to take some pictures of her," Brenna says. "I'm thinking of starting a summer business— Pet Portraits by Brenna. What do you think?"

"Well, you're in the right place to get some business," I say.

When we all went to Florida to help out with the manatees, Brenna took her camera everywhere.

She's really getting good at photography.

I watch as she moves around, taking pictures of the poodle from several different angles.

Then she turns around and looks at me. "Hey, want me to take a few shots of you and Sneakers?"

"Sure," I say. I finger-comb my hair as I kneel down beside Sneakers, then lick my lips and smile. Maybe I can send a copy to my mom with the caption: "Zoe—Friendly, housebroken, needs a good home."

"Sit!" I say to Sneakers through my posed grin.

The poodle sits. Sneakers does not. Instead, he barks and runs around my legs.

"Think you're cute?" I snort and scoop the rascal into my arms, intending to scold him. But then Sneakers licks my nose, and I can't help but laugh.

I hear Brenna's camera clicking away.

"He's cute, all right," I grudgingly admit. I hold him up beside my face, pressing my cheek against his. "But he's driving me crazy!"

"What's wrong?" Brenna asks as she snaps some more shots.

"He won't follow my commands. He absolutely refuses to learn any tricks. And he goes to the bathroom wherever and whenever he wants."

"Sounds like he has a mind of his own."

"I hadn't thought of it that way!" I laugh.

"Unfortunately, Gran seems to think his bad manners are all my fault."

"Try turning the other way," Brenna suggests. "Then hold Sneakers up and look over your shoulder at me."

I try the pose—and shriek when Sneakers pulls my hair with his teeth.

"Maybe you should try an alarm or timer," Brenna suggests, still snapping pics. "You can set it to remind you to take Sneakers out every two hours. That's what my family does when we're working with a wild animal that's sick or hurt. We set a timer to remind us to feed it and check on it. Once you've got him trained, you can gradually lengthen the time between trips."

"That might work."

"Speaking of time, I have to go. Good luck with Sneakers!" Brenna takes the poodle back into the clinic, and I hurry upstairs to my room with Sneakers in tow. He jumps onto the bed and makes himself comfy as I open my jewelry box and pull out the watch Mom gave me for my birthday last year. It has all kinds of gizmos on it. I strap it on, then fiddle with it till I figure out how to set the alarm.

I set it to beep every two hours.

Then I turn back to Sneakers. "Oh, no!" I wail.

Sneakers barks up at me—from the middle of a wet spot in the center of my bed!

Things have been pretty busy at the clinic this afternoon. The phone keeps ringing, and a steady parade of patients flows through the waiting room. Sunita, David, Brenna, and I have been helping Gran and Dr. Gabe. There's no time to check on Yum-Yum or to ask Gran how he's doing.

I'm actually glad when Maggie comes home from basketball camp. We can use her help.

I'm surprised that two hours have passed each time the alarm on my watch beeps. But when it does, I excuse myself as soon as I can and escort Sneakers, the Amazing Peeing Puppy, outdoors.

Each time, he looks up at me expectantly.

"Well?" I say. I scowl at Sneakers, trying to act tough. But he only lies down on the ground and thumps his tail.

"You're hopeless!" I scold him. Then I feel sorry for scolding him and scoop him up for a big hug.

At the end of the day, as the sun begins to set, I take Yum-Yum out to do his business. And guess who copies him?

Sneakers! He follows Yum-Yum around, goes

where he goes, then lies down beside him on the deck.

Laughing, I sit down on the top step and give both dogs a good petting, nose to tail.

I look out across the yard, listening to the birds and crickets, watching the sky explode into a dozen shades of pink and blue. A soft breeze lifts my hair and cools the perspiration on my neck.

Not a skyscraper or a taxi in sight.

"I'm a long way from Manhattan," I whisper to the dogs.

Then Gran comes out and sits down beside me. "Whew, what a day," she says.

I study her profile as she drinks in the peaceful view of the sunset. Sometimes I can hardly believe she and my mom are related, much less mother and daughter. I mean, I love them both, but they seem as different as night and day.

Gran is a tall woman, with strong hands and arms. She runs a lot and wears her hair cut super-short because she says she has no time for blow-dryers and styling gels. She's tough and serious, though kind, and would rather work in the clinic than do anything else in the world.

Mom, on the other hand, spends half her life doing her hair and makeup and working out to stay slim so she'll look great in her clothes. "It's my job to look good," she always says.

I can't help but wonder about the two of them.

"So," I ask hesitantly, "what's the news?"

"About Yum-Yum?" she asks, though of course she knows that's what I mean. Her shoulders seem to sag a little, and she sighs. "I did the biopsy and a few other tests."

"And?" *Everything's fine,* I e-mail her mentally. *Tell me everything's fine.*

"And I need to discuss the results with Jane in the morning," she says simply.

"But what do you think—"

"In the morning," she repeats firmly as she gets to her feet. Then she smiles. "Come on. I need to get out of the office. What do you say we take a drive and get some takeout? Chinese, maybe?"

"Sounds good, but Maggie will probably complain," I try to joke, picking up Sneakers to carry him inside.

But I don't really feel like eating, not even Chinese, one of my favorite kinds of food.

Wouldn't Gran tell me if Yum-Yum was okay?

SIX

*B*eep-beep-beep-beep!

I cover my head with a pillow.

Beep-beep-beep-beep!

My hand snakes out. I blindly search for the alarm clock on my nightstand. Got to hit that snooze button . . .

Then I remember.

It's not my alarm clock. It's that beeper on my watch!

I throw back my covers. I sling one foot over the side of the bed. But I can't get up. I can't even force my eyes to open.

I've never been so tired in all my life. And it's all that mangy mutt's fault!

I tried Brenna's suggestion. I took Sneakers out every two hours. Every time the beeper rang. All night long!

I didn't even bother putting him in his portable dog crate when I came back in the last time. Gran says that when you're training new puppies, it's a good place to have them sleep. She says it helps housebreak them, because they don't want to pee in their own bed. And it keeps them from wandering around at night unsupervised. But Sneakers whined too much when I put him in the crate, and I was too tired to argue!

Who would have thought something so cuddly could be so much trouble?

At last the watch stops beeping. I listen hard for sounds of Sneakers. All's quiet. I guess even he's worn out!

Maybe I'll just lie here a minute. Practice my mental telepathy—with my eyes closed, of course.

I mentally e-mail my mom: *Come get me! Save me from this endless poop patrol!*

No reply.

I send Yum-Yum a mental get-well card: *Be okay!*

I even try communicating with Sneakers by ESP. *Today you will be instantly and thoroughly trained.*

Suddenly I hear Maggie shriek down the hall.

I jump out of bed and reach the door before I'm totally awake.

Maggie is there, shoving something in my face. I open one eye and peer at it. It looks like a twisted piece of plastic.

"No, thank you," I mumble. "I can't eat when I first get up."

Maggie doesn't laugh at my joke. "When are you going to start taking care of that dog of yours?" she yells.

A surge of anger wakes me up. I mean, I've been up most of the night dog training while she snored away in her room. "What do you think I've been doing all night?" I shoot back. "I took Sneakers out every two hours. I guarantee he's on empty! If you've got poop in your room, it's definitely not ours!"

Sneakers comes running down the hall at that moment. I lean down and pat him on the head.

"I'm not talking about that," Maggie replies angrily. "I'm talking about *this!*" She shakes the icky piece of plastic in my face again. "It's my mouth guard! He chewed it to bits. And I don't have time to get a new one before camp."

Oops. Guess I left my door open when I came in that last time.

Guess Sneakers wandered a bit when I didn't put him in his crate.

"You shouldn't have let him run loose during the night," Maggie says.

"But he was whining," I say, defending myself. "I couldn't sleep—"

"He needs to stay in his crate at night—no matter how much he whines," Maggie replies. "Don't you know anything?"

I hear Gran coming down the hall. "Girls, girls, what's going on?" she asks.

"Zoe let Sneakers chew up my mouth guard," Maggie says.

"I didn't *let* him," I protest, then add, "And maybe if you didn't leave your junk all over the floor, Sneakers wouldn't have chewed it up." I knew that would make her mad. Maggie's not the neatest person in the world.

"She left Sneakers out of his crate!" Maggie says.

Gran takes the twisted lump of plastic from Maggie's hand. I expect her to give Maggie a lecture about cleaning up her room.

Instead she says, "Girls, Sneakers could have choked on this." She doesn't yell, but I feel horrible anyway. How many times have I seen her deal with pets that've swallowed harmful objects?

I take my misery out on Sneakers. "See how

much trouble you get me into?" I shout.

Sneakers looks up at me—and pees on the floor.

I can't believe it. After all the trips outside? "What do I have to do?" I explode. "Camp out all night?"

Sneakers yips and runs down the stairs.

"Good one," Maggie says.

Gran sighs. "Zoe," she explains calmly, "part of the reason Sneakers just relieved himself is that he's feeling stressed by all the yelling. And he's feeling a little intimidated by your anger."

"I'm sorry, Gran, really," I say. "But it's just so frustrating."

"Imagine how frustrated Sneakers feels," Maggie cracks.

I open my mouth to yell at my cousin, but Gran holds up a warning finger. "Why don't we start the morning over, girls, hmm?"

"But what about my mouth guard?" Maggie objects.

"Check in the kitchen, second drawer next to the fridge," Gran says calmly. "I bought an extra one."

"Gran! You're the best!" Maggie dashes off down the hall.

Gran grins. "She has a habit of misplacing them."

"I'm really sorry, Gran," I say. "About everything."

"I know, Zoe," Gran replies gently. "Training a young puppy is not the easiest thing in the world. But Sneakers will catch on. You've just got to stick with it and be consistent in your training, okay?"

I nod.

"And put him in his crate when you can't keep an eye on him. That's what it's for."

I nod again.

Gran starts to say something else, but then she glances at her watch. "Oh, I'm late! I need to go over to the clinic. Jane's coming in early to talk about Yum-Yum."

Immediately all my anger disappears—replaced by fear. But Gran is gone before I can ask her anything.

I dress quickly and head down to the kitchen. While Maggie grabs another artificially colored breakfast, I tiptoe into the clinic. I *have* to know if Yum-Yum is all right.

Gran and Jane are in the Dolittle Room. I hear their voices—Jane's is high and worried, but Gran's is deep and reassuring. Yes! That must mean Yum-Yum is all right. Gran must be telling Jane that he's going to be okay!

But Gran's next words aren't reassuring. I hear her say something horrible. "I'm sorry, Jane, but the biopsy I took confirms that the tumor in Yum-Yum's mouth is malignant melanoma."

Jane gasps.

Oh, no! That means cancer!

"No!" I cry, bursting into the room.

Gran looks up, surprised. Jane has her face in her hands, crying softly.

I grab the box of tissues on the counter and offer it to Jane. I don't know what else to do. She smiles at me a little and takes one to dab her eyes. I take one for myself, too.

"I can't believe it," Jane says tearfully. She turns to Gran with a stricken look on her face. "Is it something I did wrong, J.J.?"

"Jane! You know it's not." Gran squeezes her friend's hand. "You've always taken wonderful care of Yum-Yum. He's lucky to have you. One of the reasons we see more cancer in dogs these days is that we're taking better care of them, so they live longer. All dogs are at greater risk of developing cancer when they're more than ten or eleven years old."

"I just feel so guilty," Jane says. "Yum-Yum's my best friend, J.J. I'm with him every day. I should have noticed something was wrong. I should have known he was sick."

"You can't blame yourself," Gran insists. "Dogs hide it. The symptoms are often vague until the disease has progressed."

"I want to do chemotherapy," Jane says suddenly, her eyes flaring with hope. "I mean, they do that on dogs these days, right?"

"Yes, it's much more common than it used to be," Gran says.

"I've seen it work wonders with the kids at the hospital," Jane insists.

Gran nods.

"But . . . I've heard it costs a lot, too." Jane twists her tissue, studying the floor.

"Jane, you know how I feel about Yum-Yum," Gran says. "He's a real champ—one of my favorite patients. And it really hurts to be the one to have to tell you all this. But you know I've always been straight with you. And I think it's easier for us to deal with this if we know the truth."

Jane forces a smile through her tears. "Tell me, J.J.," she says softly. "I want to know."

"I suspect that the cancer has already spread," Gran says. Her voice is an amazing mixture of sympathy and professionalism. "And if that's true, it's too late for surgery. Removing the tumor in Yum-Yum's mouth wouldn't get rid of all the cancer. But chemotherapy might give you a little more time."

For a long time, Jane doesn't say anything. Her hands have stopped twisting and lie motionless in her lap. Gran waits patiently, giving her friend the time to let things sink in. I sit there, too, unable to move.

Suddenly Jane sits up in her chair and stares straight at Gran with a look of fire in her eyes. "I don't care how much it costs, J.J. Not if it will *save* Yum-Yum."

Gran slips an arm around Jane's shoulders. For a moment, she doesn't say anything. But her eyes are filled with sympathy, and I see her jaw clench as she works out in her mind which words to use. I can tell this is hard for her—harder than usual, because Jane is such a close friend.

When she speaks, her voice is gentle, but firm. "Jane. You have to understand. Nothing will save Yum-Yum."

I swallow hard.

"I'm sorry," Gran continues, "but I don't want to offer you false hope. Even if the chemotherapy treatments are successful—and they don't work for all dogs—they won't cure Yum-Yum. They'll only prolong his life a little longer. At the most, they'll give him another ten months to a year."

"I don't care, J.J.!" Jane says tearfully. "He's . . . he's my family. He's all I've got."

The tears well up in my eyes again.

Gran pats Jane on the arm.

Jane takes a deep breath, then asks, "Will the treatments hurt him?"

I think of that character on my mom's soap opera, the one who got cancer. The chemo treatments made her throw up a lot.

"Well, for some reason, dogs seem to tolerate chemotherapy better than people do," Gran says. "But there are always risks with this kind of treatment. And there can be side effects."

I think of Yum-Yum's silky coat. And the bald kids at the hospital. "Will he lose his hair?" I ask.

Gran smiles. "Actually, most dogs don't lose much hair at all. There may be some hair loss, but not like with people."

"Tell me, J.J.," Jane asks. "What are the alternatives?"

Gran takes a deep breath. "With no treatment, Yum-Yum doesn't have much time left. It's difficult to be exact. But at most, I'd say . . . one, maybe two months."

Jane gasps. "That's all?"

Gran nods. "It happens pretty fast, I'm afraid. I

could give him medicine to make him more comfortable." She pauses a moment, and what she says next chills me to the bone. "And, of course, putting him to sleep is another alternative."

"No," Jane whispers.

"It's not easy, but it can be a very kind thing to do for a pet who's seriously ill," Gran says.

Jane vigorously shakes her head. "But I couldn't, J.J. I just couldn't put him down."

"It's not an easy thing to do," Gran says again.

Jane sits up then and blows her nose. A determined look comes over her face. "Thanks for being straight with me, J.J. I know you have Yum-Yum's best interest at heart. But I've made up my mind. I love Yum-Yum too much. I can't just sit around and do nothing while he . . . " She can't finish the sentence. "You understand, don't you, J.J.? I . . . I have to try."

"Sure," Gran says with a reassuring smile. "A lot of people feel the same way you do."

"So, what do we do now?" Jane asks. I can see a little of her old spunkiness returning. "Can you do whatever we have to do here, at the clinic?"

Gran shakes her head. "I want to send you and Yum-Yum to the university—to the veterinary hospital there. I know it's a bit of a drive, but they have cancer specialists there. He'll get the most up-to-date treatment available." Gran gets up. "Here. I've got some information for you to read. . ."

I slip out of the office and scoot down the hall to where Yum-Yum has been sleeping in a cage.

He wags his tail when he sees me. "Hello, Yum-Yum," I say cheerfully, and he barks back. Poor darling! He has no idea what's going on or what lies ahead. I can't believe this is happening to him! He's one of the best dogs in the whole world. And he doesn't just make Jane's life happier. He makes those kids at the hospital laugh and forget their troubles. He really makes a difference in their world. And now this has to happen to him. What crummy luck! It's so unfair!

And suddenly I understand the look I saw in Emma Morgan's eyes.

SEVEN

Sherlock, sit!" Maggie commands.

The basset hound's rear end hits the ground.

Maggie turns toward me, a smug smile on her freckled face, a challenge in her gray eyes.

Something inside of me ignites. It's Saturday morning, and we're out in the yard. Maggie's been told by Gran to give me some extra help with my dog training.

But she'd better watch out, because I'm mad at the world. Mad that a wonderful dog like Yum-Yum has to get sick.

I'm determined now to train Sneakers. And I know I need help. But I think my red-haired cousin is using this as an opportunity to show off instead.

Okay, so she grew up with animals and I didn't. So she's been able to watch Gran work in the clinic all these years. So she's ahead of me when it comes to understanding animals.

But there's one thing Maggie doesn't realize about me that she's about to learn: I'm very competitive. At the private school I went to in Manhattan, I got straight A's and was known as "the girl to beat." Mom raised me to shine, and I worked hard never to disappoint her.

So if Maggie wants to play that game with me, all I can say to her is, *Hope you're not a sore loser.*

"Okay. We can do that." I turn to Sneakers. "Okay, sweetie pie," I coax. "Let's show 'em. Sit, now. Come on. Do it!"

Sneakers just stands there, wagging his tail, looking up at me like he's totally confused.

I can feel Maggie staring at me, and my face grows hot. Frustrated, I speak to Sneakers more sternly. "Sit! Sit!" I say.

Sneakers chases a squirrel up into a tree.

Maggie snickers. I ignore her. I stride over to the tree to retrieve my pooch.

"Sherlock," Maggie continues like a command sergeant in the U.S. Marines. "Lie down." She makes a motion with her hand.

Sherlock's short legs slide out in front of him till he's lying on the ground.

I get Sneakers' attention and say, "Lie down!"

Sneakers sits.

I shove my hair behind my ear and get down on my knees. "Come on, Sneak. Please?" I whisper. "You're making me look bad here." More loudly, I say, "Lie down!" I tug at his front paws, trying to make him lie flat.

Sneakers yips and tries to pull away.

Maggie clucks her tongue. Then she gives Sherlock another order. "Stay." She holds her hand out like a traffic cop telling cars to stop.

Then she walks away.

I can't believe it—Sherlock stays exactly where he is. Like his bottom's glued to the ground!

Then, very quietly, Maggie says, "Come!"

Sherlock bounds across the grass, his long ears flopping.

"Good dog!" Maggie cries, giving Sherlock a hug. "You're the best dog in the world!"

If I were a dog, I'd be growling at them. But I won't give up. I face my puppy sternly. "Stay," I say as I begin to back away.

Sneakers gets up.

"No, sit!"

Sneakers heads toward me.

"No, no!" I shout.

Sneakers runs off across the yard.

"Come back here!" I cry as I chase after him.

Sneakers circles around the yard and hides under the deck.

Panting, I blow the stray strands of hair out of my eyes and frown at Maggie. "It's not fair!"

"What?!" she exclaims.

"It's not fair," I say. "Sherlock's old. You've had years to train him."

"Oh, brother," Maggie says.

"And how do I know you didn't have somebody else teach him all these tricks in the first place?" I realize I'm kind of shouting, but I'm angry. Maggie has had Sherlock forever, and Sneakers is just a puppy.

"The only problem with Sneakers is lack of a good teacher," Maggie says. "You send him mixed signals. He doesn't know what to do." She mimics me in a high, silly voice. "Come. No! Don't! Do! Stay. Stop!"

"Stop that!" I shout, even though I have to force myself not to laugh. "I don't sound like that."

Maggie's laughing now. "Yeah, you do."

"No, I don't!" I insist hotly. "And besides, Sneakers is just a mutt. Maybe it's harder for him to learn."

Maggie scowls. "Maybe that's the problem," she says. "Maybe to you, he's 'just a mutt.' Maybe he's not fancy and expensive enough for you to really care about!"

"That's not true!" I shout.

"Girls! Girls!" Gran comes striding out of the clinic.

Maggie and I instantly stop fighting.

"Hi, Gran," I say cheerfully. "What's up?"

"I can hear you both howling like wet cats all the way inside the clinic!" she says.

"It's Zoe's fault," Maggie instantly replies. "She's—"

"Maggie's being rude," I insist.

"Hold it!" Gran holds up both hands in front of her. "I've had enough of you two fighting. Maggie, inside."

"But, Gran—"

"Now. Before you two say things you'll be sorry about later."

Maggie sulks and heads toward the house. "Sherlock, come!"

When the basset hound follows instantly, Maggie shoots me a triumphant look. Then they disappear inside the house.

Gran turns toward me.

"I'm sorry, Gran, but Maggie is just so—"

"Why don't you take a walk, Zoe."

"But, Gran—"

"Take a walk, Zoe. It'll do you good. And take Sneakers with you. On a leash. That's the only way to train a dog."

With a sigh, I find Sneakers' leash. At least I don't have to put up with Maggie's put-downs anymore.

Then Sneakers and I take off. I'm so charged up, I walk really fast. Sneakers seems to enjoy it. We walk for twenty minutes without slowing down.

I decide to stop by Jane's salon to see how she and Yum-Yum are doing.

When I walk by the window, Jane comes to the door and waves to me. Her eyes look red, as if she's been crying. But she gives me a smile. "Come on in."

I start to tie Sneakers to a bike rack out front, but Jane calls out, "Oh, don't be silly. This is a dog-friendly salon. Bring him in!"

"Are you sure?"

Jane nods and waves us in. "Sure I'm sure. Come on inside!"

Sneakers and I go in.

"I was just sweeping up from my last customer," Jane says as she picks up the broom. She's already swept up a huge pile of silvery blond hair.

"It's almost enough to make another Yum-Yum,"

I joke—without thinking.

Jane just smiles wistfully as she sweeps the hair into a dustpan. "Listen, Zoe," she says as she dumps the hair in the trash. "I talked to the staff of the children's hospital. I—I'd like to take Yum-Yum in to say good-bye to the kids because . . ." She forces a cheerful smile. "Because it might be a while before he can go back to see all his fans."

"I'm sure they'll be glad to see him," I say.

Jane nods, then cocks her head to one side and stares at Sneakers. "You know, Zoe, Sneakers is really so cute. And look how well he's behaving."

It's true. He's sitting there beside me like a true little gentleman. It's probably because he's worn out from our walk, but I don't mention that.

"You know what we could do?"

"What?"

She shrugs casually. "We could take Sneakers along to the hospital with us."

"Sneakers?" I say in disbelief. "You've got to be kidding!"

Jane laughs. "Yes, Sneakers. He's a wonderful dog, and I think he has real potential. Normally you have to take a dog through a training program before he's allowed to go into the hospital on a regular basis," Jane explains. "But the folks on the children's ward are pretty happy to get any kind of help in cheering up those kids. I don't think they'd mind a quick little visit, just to see if you and Sneakers like it. Who knows? You might decide you want to do formal training. Come on—what do you think?"

What do I think? I'm not sure. I look at that rascal Sneakers and wonder if he can do it. If *I* can do it.

But then Sneakers barks, and the sound is so cheerful and full of life.

Maybe he could do some good. Maybe he could even make Emma laugh.

Wouldn't that show Maggie and Gran!

"Come on, Sneakers!" I say. "Let's give it a try!"

What a cute little dog!" Nurse Bennett says when we arrive at the hospital. "You know, we usually only let in trained therapy pets. Although sometimes we let parents bring in a child's pet."

"We won't stay long," Jane says. "But if things go well, we might have a new therapy dog in training here."

"That we can sure use!" Nurse Bennett says. "All right, just this once."

I cross my fingers for luck and smile down at my dog. So far Sneakers is behaving perfectly, copying Yum-Yum's every move. Yum-Yum is trying his best to put on a good show, but he seems a little tired.

"Do you have any advice on how I should talk to the kids about Yum-Yum's cancer?" Jane asks.

"Well, we've broken the news to them already," Nurse Bennett says. "They're pretty upset about it.

But these kids have seen it all. So mostly, I'd say just answer their questions honestly."

I brace myself for a really sad time.

But as we walk down the hall, kids stream out of their rooms to greet Yum-Yum. They've made him get-well cards and posters. Everyone seems to want to hold him and talk to him and give him advice about his treatment.

Jane is as amazed as I am. "I guess in some ways, they feel even closer to Yum-Yum than before—since they share the same disease."

The kids are happy to meet Yum-Yum's "good buddy Sneakers," too. I cross my fingers again. So far Sneakers is behaving himself—and loving all the attention. He doesn't bark much, and it doesn't seem to bother him at all to have lots of kids petting him and trying to hug him.

I look around for Emma Morgan. I want to try to talk to her again. I want her to meet Sneakers.

I see her across the room, in her usual spot. But instead of staring out the window, she's looking at me—waiting for me. I wave and start to go over, but a little girl steps in front of me and yanks on my shirt. I realize it's the same little girl who put clips in Yum-Yum's hair.

"Hi, Stephanie."

"Hi . . . um, what was your name?"

"Zoe. Remember I came with Yum-Yum a few days ago?"

She nods sadly. "I'm so sorry that Yum-Yum is sick."

"Yeah, me too."

Then Stephanie's face lights up. "Do you think Sneakers would let me brush him?" she asks. "Do you think he'd let me put some clips in his hair?"

I smile at the little girl. I remember being her age. I remember being obsessed with brushing and braiding and doing all kinds of things to my dolls' hair. Sometimes my mom even used to let me do weird experiments on her hair.

But Stephanie doesn't have any hair to braid.

Actually, Sneakers doesn't have that much, either. Not like Yum-Yum. "Well, Sneakers' hair is pretty short," I say. "I don't know if the clips will stay in."

Stephanie cocks her head and thinks a minute. "I know!" She takes a purple scrunchie and loops it over Sneakers' left ear. She slips a hot-pink one onto his tail. "Sneakers!" she squeals. "You're bee-yoo-ti-ful!"

Sneakers runs around in a circle, trying to catch the bright pink cloth on his tail.

Stephanie chases him.

Another little girl sees them and joins in the game.

Sneakers is getting excited. He jumps up on one of the nurses.

"Down, Sneakers!" I tell him.

But he won't listen. The more I call him, it seems, the more he ignores me.

He runs up to the nurses' desk with kids chasing after him.

Oh, no! He's not going to . . . "No! Sneakers!"

He tinkles right in the middle of the floor.

"I'm so sorry," I say to Nurse Bennett, and I can feel my face turning bright red. "Do you have any paper towels?"

She shakes her head. "I'll take care of it." She sighs and glances at Jane. "Sorry, Jane, but . . . maybe it would just be best for you to take Sneakers outside."

I'm totally embarrassed. I glance back at Emma. She has turned her chair away from the whole scene. She won't look at either dog.

She won't even wave good-bye.

As Jane and I walk back to the car with our dogs, I apologize over and over.

"Don't be silly," she says. "He just got excited, that's all. But you see, that's why the special training is so important. If you and Sneakers take the formal training classes, you and he will learn how to behave in all kinds of new situations."

Jane is being so nice, but I feel so humiliated. Sneakers and I aren't like Jane and Yum-Yum—we're a terrible team. And I don't see therapy training in our future at all.

"Promise me one thing," I beg her as I slink into the car. "Don't tell Maggie or Gran!"

NINE

It's an hour-long drive to the university vet hospital where Jane is taking Yum-Yum for cancer treatments. Gran said she wished she could go with Jane, but she's got her hands full at the clinic, with Dr. Gabe on vacation. So I volunteered to go.

I hold Yum-Yum in my lap as we drive out of town and into the country, past rolling hills and old family farms.

I notice round, colorful folk-art designs on signs over the doors of some of the barns. "What are those things?" I ask.

"Pennsylvania Dutch hex signs," she explains. "Aren't they beautiful? The Germans brought them over from the Old Country. They're supposed to keep away evil spirits."

We could use a good-luck charm like that ourselves today.

Yum-Yum squirms a little, as if he can't get comfortable. I stroke him softly, and he seems to settle down.

I try to entertain Jane, to keep her from worrying. I tell her about what it was like living in Manhattan, a place she's only seen on television and in the movies. "I wish you could meet my mom," I say. "You'd really like her."

"I feel like I know her already."

"How?" I ask, puzzled.

"From watching her soap on TV, silly!" Jane laughs. "I tuned in to watch the show when your grandmother first told me about Rose being on TV. Then I got so hooked on the show, I couldn't stop watching! I always used to have it on in my shop, and all my customers got stuck on it, too." Jane shakes her head and smiles. "I'll never forget that first episode. Rose only had a few lines that day, but your grandmother and I gave her a standing ovation. J.J. was so proud of her!"

"Really?" I say. "I didn't know that." I don't think my mom knows that, either. Somehow I always got the feeling that Gran didn't approve of Mom's acting.

"You look just like her," Jane says.

That makes me smile.

Jane sighs. "The day the last episode ran, a couple

of my regulars and I just sat in front of the TV and cried. We couldn't believe they'd canceled that show."

"I couldn't believe it, either," I say softly.

Jane shoots me a quick glance, then reaches over and squeezes my hand. "Tough break for you, too, huh, kiddo?" she says.

I nod. "It's hard . . ." I don't finish my sentence, but Jane seems to understand what I mean.

"Don't worry," she says cheerfully. "Your mom's young and gorgeous, and unlike a lot of those soap stars, she can actually act. She'll get something fabulous going before you know it, and then the two of you will be back together again." She pats my hand, then says with a little catch in her voice, "Meanwhile, Yum-Yum and I are really glad you're here."

And it hits me—even though I miss Mom really badly, I'm glad I'm here, too.

Glancing down, I realize that Yum-Yum has fallen asleep, and I study the little dog in my arms. He looks the same as always—tiny and plump, with a cute little nose half-hidden by long, silky hair. I brushed him well today before coming so he'd look his best. Jane dressed him up with a bright red bow.

If I didn't already know how sick he is, there'd be

no way to tell from looking at him. It's hard to imagine the illness spreading secretly through his body.

Maybe he's not all that sick yet. Maybe we've caught it early, and they'll be able to make him well. I make a wish on all the hex signs we pass along the way.

Finally we reach the cancer center. As we get out of the car, I can tell Jane is nervous.

"Don't worry, Jane," I say as I gently pass Yum-Yum into her arms. "Gran says the doctors here are the best."

Jane shakes her head. "J.J.'s the best. But if she recommends these folks, I'm sure they'll be great."

Inside we check in at the front desk, then get sent to a waiting area. It's a lot like the waiting room at Gran's—only much, much bigger. Lots of people are waiting with their pets. Some of the animals don't look sick at all. Others look tired and weak.

I wonder what's wrong with them. I wonder if some of them have cancer like Yum-Yum.

At last a tall woman in a white coat comes out to meet us. "Ms. Young?"

Jane looks scared. "Yes?"

"Hi, I'm Dr. Edwards. I understand you're a

friend of J.J. MacKenzie's." She holds out a hand for Yum-Yum to sniff. "And Dr. Mac's taking care of little Yum-Yum here, huh?"

Yum-Yum wags his tail and licks Dr. Edwards' hand.

Jane seems to relax. I guess she thinks if Dr. Edwards passes the Yum-Yum test, she's all right.

When Dr. Edwards looks over at me, I hold out my hand. "I'm Zoe, Dr. Mac's granddaughter."

Dr. Edwards smiles and takes my hand. "I'm glad to meet you. Your grandmother is a good friend— and a great vet. Well, come on. Let's go have a look at Yum-Yum."

The patient room is a lot like the one back at Gran's clinic. Somehow I expected a top cancer treatment center to look more high-tech—more like *Star Trek* or something. But as Gran told me once, "Medicine is in the minds and hands of the doctors and nurses—not in the clinic's interior design."

Dr. Edwards examines Yum-Yum with quick, sure hands, feeling all over his body, the way Gran did. She takes his temperature and some blood samples.

"I'd like to do a fine-needle biopsy of one of Yum-Yum's lymph nodes," Dr. Edwards says.

"Can I stay while you do it?" Jane asks.

"Sure," she replies.

They don't ask me, but since Jane is clutching my hand so tightly it's cutting off my circulation, I figure I'll stay.

Dr. Edwards explains that this biopsy can be done while Yum-Yum is awake. While Jane holds him, Dr. Edwards inserts a thin needle into one of the lymph nodes. She explains that as she pulls up on the syringe, it removes some of the cells, which she can then examine under a microscope.

I can't believe how good Yum-Yum is through the whole thing.

Then Dr. Edwards shoos us out of the office, and we have to do some waiting, which is hard on Jane. But soon Dr. Edwards calls us back into her office to talk.

Jane looks as if she has a million questions. But she just clutches her shoulder bag as she waits for the doctor to speak.

"We don't have all the tests back," Dr. Edwards begins.

And somehow I already know the news isn't good.

"But the biopsy shows that the cancer has spread from the original tumor in Yum-Yum's mouth to the lymph nodes, just as Dr. Mac suspected." Dr. Edwards' face is serious, professional, but also very kind. "It's spreading into the jaw and damaging the teeth."

"Not good, huh?" Jane says, her voice barely a whisper. Her eyes beg to be contradicted.

"Not good," Dr. Edwards agrees gently. "From my examination, he seems to be experiencing some pain already. But he's a tough little dog," she adds with a smile.

"I should have done something sooner," Jane says. "I should have realized he was sick."

Dr. Edwards shakes her head. "You saw Dr. Mac as soon as you noticed something wrong. That was the most anyone could have done. This is a rapid disease, Jane—and a sneaky one—in both animals and people."

Something in Dr. Edwards' eyes tells me that maybe she's lost a loved one to cancer.

"What about chemotherapy? Is it too late to try that?" Jane asks.

"No, we can still try that," Dr. Edwards says. "We're having a lot of success with chemotherapy for dogs. Most dogs handle the treatments well. But I'm sure Dr. Mac has explained to you that what we do here is not a cure. The best we can do is work our hardest to arrest the disease—to keep it from spreading. After a complete series of treatments, a good many of our animals go into remission—which means there are no outward signs of the disease. But even then, remission for most animals only lasts about ten to twelve months—sometimes less, sometimes more. Each type of cancer responds differently to chemotherapy and unfortunately, we have less success with Yum-Yum's type of tumor."

Jane nods her head. "Tell me about the treatments," she says simply.

Dr. Edwards hands some printed sheets across the desk, but Jane doesn't move to pick them up. She just listens to the doctor's words.

"Many of the drugs we use to treat cancer in animals are the same drugs that are used on people. A normal course of treatment would be four to six rounds of chemotherapy, at three-week intervals. We also like to see the animal every week for four weeks, then a little less often after that."

Jane stares out the window. When she turns back to the doctor, her eyes are watery, but her expression is calm. "Is it worth it, Dr. Edwards?"

Dr. Edwards sighs wistfully and shakes her head. "That's a very difficult question to answer, Jane. I have two dogs myself." She points to a photograph on her desk of a pair of beautiful golden retrievers. "Morgan and MacDougal. They're very special to me. And working here, of course, I've thought about what I'd do myself. But it's a very individual decision, Jane, one that no one can make for you."

Dr. Edwards leans forward across her desk. "Every dog—just like every person—is unique, and we have to deal with each case in a different way. Chemotherapy will be a big investment on your part—an investment of money, an investment of time, and an emotional investment, too. Many dogs do well under chemotherapy, and we're able to extend their lives by many months. We can even cure some cancers. But if it becomes clear that the treatment is not working, that your animal is in pain or severe discomfort, we will inform you of that. Only you can decide what you want for Yum-Yum."

She swivels in her chair and nods at me. "We hope, by the time this young woman is grown, to have this stuff under control—if not totally cured. But for now, Jane, this is the best we can offer."

"What's best for Yum-Yum," Jane says. "That's what I want."

"It's your decision. But I would urge you to try to come to a decision as soon as possible. Now— today—if you can. If you do decide to do the chemotherapy, we don't want to waste any time. We should go ahead and start—this afternoon."

"Can I have a few minutes?" Jane asks.

Dr. Edwards smiles. "Of course. I'm going to check on another patient. Then I'll be right back." She gets up and leaves the office, closing the door behind her to give Jane privacy.

Jane holds Yum-Yum in her arms and gazes out the window.

I decide to give her some time alone, too. I move toward the door. "I think I'm going to go look for a soda machine," I say softly. "Can I bring you anything?"

"No thanks, dear," Jane says, without looking up.

I head out to the front desk and ask the nurse if there are any snack machines around. I follow her directions, digging change out of my pockets. I walk very, very slowly.

Jane has a lot to think about. I want to give her all the time in the world.

When I get back with my soda, Jane is sitting in the waiting room. Things have happened fast.

"Where's Yum-Yum?" I ask.

Jane reaches out for my hand. "I decided to go ahead with the chemo," she says. "To see if I can give him a few more months of quality time." She looks at me, and this time her eyes are strangely dry. "I hope I did the right thing, Zoe. I just feel like I have to at least try."

I reach over and give her a hug. "Yum-Yum is lucky to have you," I whisper into her shoulder. She squeezes me hard, then lets me go.

"So now what happens?" I ask.

"Yum-Yum's in there now, getting his first treatment."

"Won't they let you be with him?" I ask. "You should insist!"

Jane shakes her head. "The chemotherapy drugs are given through an I.V. You know what that is, don't you?"

I nod. Since I've been at the clinic, I've seen Gran do it. It's a way to inject a liquid drug through a needle directly into a vein.

"They say it's very important for the dog to stay completely still during the treatment," Jane continues. "They say it's actually easier on the animal if the owner isn't there. They'll have someone hold Yum-Yum still, but Dr. Edwards assured me that they're very kind and gentle."

"How long will it take?" I ask.

"About thirty minutes," Jane says.

That's quick. I ask her if she wants to take a walk

with me, or if she wants a magazine or some coffee.

But Jane says she just prefers to sit and wait.

So we sit. My opened soda can stands untouched on the chair beside me, losing its fizz.

The minutes drag by.

At last Dr. Edwards brings Yum-Yum out to us. At first I'm almost afraid to look at him. How has the chemotherapy affected him? But when I study him, I'm surprised to see that he looks just the same. He acts the same, too. For animals, the treatment can be as silent as the disease.

"Yum-Yum's a wonderful little patient," Dr. Edwards says. "He has the best manners I've ever seen. It made it much easier to do the treatment."

Jane beams at the compliment. She explains it's probably because he's a therapy dog.

"I bet he's terrific with his patients," Dr. Edwards adds.

Then they talk about the details of Yum-Yum's next treatments and set up a schedule. Dr. Edwards gives Jane more printed information.

Yum-Yum sits patiently through it all, wagging his tail.

+

Jane is quiet as she drives through the peaceful countryside on the way home. I hold Yum-Yum, wondering about the chemicals coursing through his blood. I try to use ESP to make the drugs work fast.

"It's kind of strange to think that Yum-Yum is going through the same things as Emma and Michael and the other kids at the hospital," I say.

Jane nods. "I know Yum-Yum will miss going in to see them."

"Maybe if he does all right with the chemo, he can still go in sometimes," I suggest. "If he's feeling okay."

"We'll see," Jane says, then adds, "I still think you should consider going through the training with Sneakers."

I laugh. "Are you kidding? You saw what he did at the hospital the other day. Sneakers is a mess! A good dog," I'm quick to add, "but a real mess."

"Psh! He's young," Jane assures me. "He just needs lots of love and a lot more training, that's all."

"I don't know, Jane," I say as I stare out the window at the fields rushing past. "I'm just no good at training him."

"Well, you must have done something right," she

says. "J.J. has told me how you all helped save Sneakers from that puppy mill. He had a really tough beginning—starved and mistreated. All that could have made him a mean or mistrustful dog. But he's not. He's very happy and loving. Part of that's his nature, but part of it's due to how he's been treated. How *you've* treated him."

I look at Jane in surprise. I hadn't thought of that. I was beginning to think I was just a big, fat failure when it came to Sneakers. Sure, I'm probably not the best dog trainer. But maybe loving Sneakers is a good start.

"Dogs learn a lot from their owners," Jane said. "And Sneakers is such a sweetheart. He's learned love and trust from you. He's learned to like and trust people instead of fear them. Hey, that's more than half the battle." She reaches over and pats me on the leg. "That's something to be proud of. Now all you've got to do is work on his manners a little."

I smile at Jane. Her words mean a lot to me. "Do you really think I can do it?" I ask.

"I know you can," she says. "Keep working with him. And if he shows he can learn, I'll help you get him enrolled in a formal training program."

I cuddle Yum-Yum in my arms. "What do you

think?" I murmur in his ear. "Think Sneakers and I can do it?"

Yum-Yum is dozing, exhausted from his day.

But he almost looks like he's smiling.

TEN

Two nights later, I'm dreaming that I'm in the circus. The audience applauds as Sneakers—dressed in a ruffly collar and a sparkling hat—leaps through a ring of fire. Proudly, I bow before a standing ovation. Sneakers sits up on his hind legs and barks.

Over and over. He keeps barking, even after the audience stops clapping. Even after the audience fades away.

Suddenly I sit up. I'm not at the circus. I'm in my bed. It's dark in my room, and Sneakers is barking wildly in his crate.

"Shhh!" I tell him. I pick up my watch from the nightstand. "Sneakers!" I whisper. "For goodness sake, it's three A.M.!"

I crawl out of bed and open the crate. Sneakers darts out and runs through the open bedroom door.

"Whoa," I say through a yawn. "He must really gotta go."

I follow him downstairs, but he's not standing by the back door. He's pawing at the door leading into the clinic.

The lights are on. Gran must be in there. *Emergency!*

I open the door, and Sneakers scampers into the clinic. I'm right behind him. Maybe Gran will need my help.

My heart skips a beat when I see who's there with her.

Jane and Yum-Yum!

"Gran! Jane! What's wrong?" I ask.

Jane looks stricken. "Yum-Yum hasn't eaten in almost two days. At first I thought the treatment might have made him lose his appetite. Then tonight, I noticed his jaw was a little funny looking. I woke up at two A.M. to his whimpering. J.J., can you help him?"

They rush him into a treatment room. I stand near the door, but I think I'm too upset to help.

Gran gently strokes the dog, examining him everywhere. He yelps when her hands barely touch his muzzle.

Gran's brow knots. "His teeth are loose, and he

may have even fractured his jaw. The tumor is doing extensive damage now," she says.

"Fractured!" Jane exclaims. "But how? I've been taking such good care of him! He's with me night and day, J.J. He hasn't fallen or tripped—"

"Jane . . ." Gran lays a hand on her friend's arm. "That's not it. I can't be sure without more tests, but I'm pretty certain that the cancer has spread to his bones."

I turn away. How awful! How will he be able to eat now? Yum-Yum's body is breaking down. And all our love can't stop it. "I'll be out in the waiting room if you need me, Gran."

Gran is kind enough not to ask me to stay.

I sit at the receptionist's desk and sort through piles of paperwork and files, trying to be useful, trying to keep my mind busy. But the words written on them blur as my eyes fill with tears. I push them to the side, afraid I'll just mess them up.

I marvel at how quiet the world seems at three A.M. People sleeping, dreaming their dreams—even as an emergency takes place down the hall.

At some point I feel someone shaking me. I realize I've fallen asleep on my folded arms, drooling into the corner of my elbow. I get up and shake the sleep from my eyes.

"How is he?" I blurt out.

"Yum-Yum is resting comfortably," Gran tells me. "I gave him something for the pain."

Jane is sitting across from me on one of the waiting room couches. She looks as if she's in a daze.

I don't know what to say or do. And I'm afraid to ask questions. "I'll go make some tea," I say, and hurry into the kitchen.

The water seems as if it will never boil, but at last it does, and I hurry back into the clinic with three mugs of tea.

I find Sneakers sitting on the couch next to Jane. She laughs softly through her tears. "That's perfect therapy dog behavior," she says, rubbing the little dog's head. "Sneakers can sense who needs some comfort."

I'm surprised. "You mean, he can really tell what you're thinking?"

"Sure," Jane says. "Sometimes I could swear Yum-Yum is reading my mind."

I think of my mom's latest craze. "You mean, like ESP and all that?"

Gran smiles. "Well, I don't know about that. But dogs are very tuned in to people. They can pick up on all kinds of little signals—expressions, body language, mood. That's why it's so easy to send the wrong signals to dogs when we train them. They just want to please humans. They need consistent, steady training. And lots of love."

Jane sits there a moment, stroking Sneakers' back. Of course, Sneakers loves it. But I realize that the action seems to help Jane even more than it does Sneakers. A calmness comes over her.

"J.J.," she says at last.

"Yes, Jane?"

Jane looks at Gran without speaking.

Gran looks back.

And I think, wow. Amazing. Neither woman says a word, and yet a whole conversation passes between them. Even watching from the outside, I know what they're saying. So their next words don't really surprise me—even though it hurts to hear them spoken aloud.

"I think if Yum-Yum could talk," Jane almost whispers, "I think he'd say . . . it's time."

Gran nods.

"I love Yum-Yum so much—" Her voice breaks.

Tears well up in the corner of Gran's eyes.

"Enough to let him go," Jane finishes.

Gran hugs Jane, and the two women just hold

each other for a moment.

Then Jane pulls away, wiping the back of her hand across her eyes.

"Oh, Jane . . ." I say. And I know. They're going to put Yum-Yum to sleep.

"You don't need me, do you, Gran?" I say as the tears stream down my face. I know there's no way I can help with this.

"No, hon. We'll be fine."

"Can I go tell him good-bye?"

Gran nods. She and Jane let me go in alone.

I go over to the cage where Yum-Yum is dozing. I open the door and stroke his soft fur. I scratch behind his ears, just the way he likes it, and his eyes flutter open a little.

"Good-bye, Yum-Yum," I whisper. "I'll never forget you." I kiss his little head.

Then I run from the room.

Gran catches me in her arms and holds me close. It helps.

Then she releases me, and she and Jane go in together. To tell Yum-Yum good-bye. And to take away his pain.

I don't know how Gran can do it. She really is amazing.

I run outside and sit on the back deck.

I watch the first whisper of pink tint the sky.

Sneakers climbs into my lap, and I hold him tightly as he licks my tears away.

ELEVEN

By the time the rest of the world yawns awake, I'm out in the yard, hard at work. I can hardly bear to think about Yum-Yum—it's too painful. It's worse if I sit and do nothing. So I throw myself into a heavy training session to block the grief from my mind.

"Sit, Sneakers. Sit."

When he doesn't sit at first, I press down gently on his rump and pull up on the leash. Sneakers instantly sits.

"Good dog!" I praise him, rubbing his ears. Sneakers barks happily.

With Sneakers' help, I've dried all my tears. And I've decided there's only one way to really deal with my sadness over Yum-Yum. That's for me and Sneakers to continue Yum-Yum's work at the hospital. It will be like a tribute to his memory. Maybe that will help.

We do "sit" a couple more times. Sneakers gets better, and each time, I reward him for doing it right.

Then I switch to "stay." I stretch out my right hand, palm forward. I move my hand right in front of his face and say firmly, "Stay. Stay!" Slowly I take one step away.

Sneakers barks happily and lunges after me.

"No, no, no!" I say, pulling up on the leash. He looks so cute that I want to reach down and hug him.

But I don't. I make myself resist the urge. I must be careful not to send him mixed signals and confuse him. And I must give him praise only when he does something right. "Let's start again with 'sit' and then 'stay.'"

I smile. It's finally sinking into my thick head that part of training a dog is training yourself. "We'll keep working on it, over and over, till we get it right—you and me, Sneakers. I promise."

We begin again.

The sun is still low in the sky when I hear the screen door screech open.

Gran has taken Jane home, so I know it's Maggie before I even turn around. I hear her bare feet on the deck.

"Whatcha doing?" she asks as she sits down on

the top step. Her hair is still rumpled from sleep.

"What does it look like?"

"Kind of early."

I shake my head. "Actually . . . it's kind of late."

"Huh?"

The sadness wells up in my throat again, but I try to keep it from spilling over. I don't want to look like a wimp in front of Maggie. "Jane Young brought Yum-Yum in last night, around three o'clock—"

"Oh, no—"

"Yeah." I sit down on the step beside my cousin to tell her what happened. "Gran had to—" My voice chokes. "You know . . ."

Incredibly, Maggie reads my mind. She's silent, clears her throat . . . and the next thing I know, she's giving me a hard hug.

Maybe my stubborn cousin and I do have something in common.

After a few seconds, we pull apart. I wipe my face with my sleeve.

"So how's Jane?" Maggie asks.

"Not too well. Gran's over there with her now."

"How're you doing?"

"I'm okay."

Maggie stares out across the yard. "That's part of being a vet volunteer. But you never get used to it.

At least, I never do. Even though I know it stops the suffering."

"Gran's amazing," I say.

Maggie nods. That's one thing she agrees with me about. "She loves animals. And that's why she's strong enough to be there for them even during the hard parts."

Sneakers trots up with a stick in his mouth.

"Oh, you want to play, huh?" I say. I pull on the stick, trying to take it away so that we can play fetch.

Sneakers won't let go.

"Hey! I can't throw it if you won't let go!" I say, tugging on the stick.

Maggie clears her throat. "Do you mind if I make a suggestion?"

She says it so nicely—so unlike the way we've talked to each other in the past week—that I have to laugh. "Please," I say.

Maggie grins and stands up. "Okay. Let go of the stick."

I let go.

"Now stand up," she orders me, and we walk down into the grass. "Think *firm*. Let him know you're the boss and that you expect him to mind."

"I'll try," I say. "But what *exactly* do I do?"

"Hold out your hand and say, 'Give.'"

I actually laugh out loud. "Yeah, right. No way that'll work!"

"It'll work," Maggie insists. "If you say it the same way each time—and keep saying it till he understands what you mean. And praise him even if he just *thinks* about giving the stick up."

"Okay." I turn toward Sneakers. I think about a teacher I had in third grade, Mrs. Myerson. I hold out my hand the way she did when she knew a kid had gum in his mouth. "Give," I say firmly.

Sneakers promptly runs off across the yard.

I glare at my cousin. "See? I told you."

"Give the dog a break," Maggie says. "It's the first time you did it."

I start to chase after Sneakers. "Come back here! Give me that—"

"Don't," Maggie says, grabbing my sleeve.

"But . . . "

Maggie grins and shakes her head. "Plant your feet. Make him come to you. Make him sit. Use your leash to keep him from running off. Insist—through your body language, the look in your eye. He'll come around."

"But—"

"Trust me," Maggie says, laughing. "The most important thing to remember is this: Dogs want to please you. Got that?" She turns back toward the deck. "Keep trying while I go make us breakfast."

"Uh, Maggie?"

"Yeah?"

"Can we maybe have something besides that fake food you call cereal?"

"Sure," Maggie says with a grin. "How about some *microwave* French toast?"

I roll my eyes, but this morning I can't argue.

My dog and I have work to do.

After breakfast, I decide to make a big chart to track my training time with Sneakers. Brenna gave me copies of the pictures she took the other day, and I pick out my favorite—the one of Sneakers licking my face—to tape to the chart. Then I write "Zoe and Sneakers' Training Chart" across the top. After all, we're both learning what to do.

I've noticed that when I work with Sneakers, he does pretty well for a while, but then he gets distracted. So I plan to work in short sessions, a couple of times a day. *Every* day.

I use a magnet to stick my chart to the refrigerator so that I won't forget about it. I don't know if it will work.

But I'm going to try.

✚

Five days later, I'm stunned. Sneakers is doing better. Even Maggie is impressed.

"See?" Maggie says. "I knew you could do it."

I smile at her praise.

"All you needed to do," Maggie adds, "was do *exactly* what I told you!"

I pretend to growl. Then I grin. "Thanks so much, *Margaret!*"

"Don't call me Margaret!" Maggie screeches. She hates that name.

Gran steps out on the deck, shaking her head. "Girls, girls. Not again. How many times—"

She stops when she sees Maggie and me laughing and throwing leaves at each other, and she smiles. "Never mind," she says, and heads back inside.

So the training is going well. Getting Sneakers to stay in his crate at night is a bit harder. The first night, I gave up and let him sleep in the bed with me, but I closed my door so that he wouldn't wander around the house. When I woke up in the morning, Sneakers was quiet—too quiet! I jumped out of bed and found him chewing on one of my shoes.

That definitely motivated me to work harder!

So that night, I put him in his crate. But the only way I could get him to stop whimpering and crying was to sleep right next to his crate with my hand where he could lick it.

I was pretty sore the next morning from sleeping on the floor.

The next night, I moved a little farther away. The following night, I put a T-shirt I'd worn that day into Sneakers' crate with him. I guess it smelled enough like me to make him happy. He was pretty quiet most of the night.

By the next night we both slept peacefully in our beds.

The one command that still doesn't work with Sneakers is "roll over." He just doesn't seem to understand what I mean. I even act it out for him. I get grass stains all over my clothes, but he still doesn't get it. I'll keep trying, though, because the kids really like it.

Two days later, I'm walking Sneakers around the neighborhood. He's doing pretty well with "heel."

Then I realize we're near the beauty salon.

Jane hasn't come by Wild at Heart since the

night they put Yum-Yum to sleep. And I haven't gone to see her, either. I guess I stayed away because I don't know what to say.

I look through the plate-glass window and see Jane blow-drying a customer's short red hair. She'll be finished soon.

"Maybe we should stop in and say hi, huh, Sneakers?"

Sneakers barks, so I lead him up the steps. A bell over the door tinkles as we enter the salon.

Still brushing and blowing, Jane looks over her shoulder. "Zoe!" she exclaims. "And Sneakers! How're you doing!"

"Hi, Jane," I say. "Are you busy?"

"Mrs. Martin here is my last customer till this evening. Can you wait?"

"Sure." I sit down next to Mrs. Martin's twins, Heidi and Holly.

"Sit," I say to Sneakers.

Sneakers sits just as prettily as a dog on TV.

"Wow," Jane says over the hum of the blow-dryer. "When did he learn that?"

"I've been working with him all week," I say.

Jane nods—it's too noisy to keep talking. So I wait. I notice framed photos of Yum-Yum on the counter, and I feel a little pinch in my heart. I mean, I still have my dog, and he's alive and well. I hope that won't make Jane feel bad that hers is gone.

The twins start petting Sneakers and talking to him. Sneakers enjoys the attention but stays where he is. If he starts to jump up on one of the kids, I will know to remind him, "Off!"

It feels great when Sneakers obeys perfectly. *What a smart dog!*

Soon Jane turns off her blow-dryer, brushes Mrs. Martin's hair a little, and holds up a mirror.

"Perfect!" Mrs. Martin says. "As always. Thanks, Jane."

Jane whisks off the cape, then goes to the cash register by the door. While Mrs. Martin pays, I show the twins some of Sneakers' tricks: "sit," "stay," and "shake."

The twins are impressed. "Hey, Mom!" Heidi shouts. "Can we get a dog like this?"

Mrs. Martin smiles. "We'll talk about it at home."

Holly pouts. "That's what she always says," she mutters.

I grin. "Tell her that mutts are very lovable."

Both kids' eyes light up. "We will!" they say.

When the Martins leave, Jane comes over to pet Sneakers. "How's my little buddy?" she coos, scratching him behind the ears, just like she always did with Yum-Yum.

Sneakers barks to say he's fine.

"I've really worked hard at training him this week," I say.

"It shows."

I'm quiet for a moment, trying to say what I don't know how to say. "I'm sorry I haven't come to see you."

Jane looks at me with a smile that seems happy and sad at the same time. "That's okay, honey. I understand. I haven't felt much like visiting this week anyway."

I don't know if this will make her feel worse, but I tell her, "I miss Yum-Yum."

The funny thing is, it seems to make her happier. She gives me a hug. "Thanks, sweetheart. A lot of people don't bother to say anything. I guess they think he was just a dog. But you know, Yum-Yum was my family."

I nod.

"I haven't been back to see the kids at the hospital," she admits. "I called the nurses to let them know what happened. Did you see the cards the kids made for me?"

She points to a bulletin board behind the desk. It's covered with dozens of handmade cards.

"Did Emma make a card?" I ask her.

Jane nods and points to a card in the middle. It's a red construction-paper heart that's been cut into two jagged pieces. A broken heart.

So Emma is paying attention! She just keeps it all inside. Obviously Yum-Yum was starting to get through to her.

"I wish I was up to going in," Jane says. "I miss going. I wonder how the kids are doing."

"Do you think you'll get another dog?" I ask. Instantly I wonder if it was the wrong thing to say.

But Jane just smiles kind of lopsidedly and shakes her head. "No. I just can't stand the thought of replacing Yum-Yum. At least, not yet. Maybe one day." She sighs. "I feel sorry about leaving the therapy program in need, though."

I nod, thinking about Emma.

Sneakers jumps up into Jane's lap, and she gives him a warm hug. Then she strokes his fur thoughtfully. "I've got an idea, Zoe. Let's take Sneakers over to the hospital again. You've been working so hard with him. Maybe he's a therapy dog after all."

"You mean, now?" I ask.

"Why not?" Jane says. "Look how well behaved he's been in here, with the twins and the noise from the blow-dryer. He's really improved. Come on.

Let's try it."

"I'm not sure," I say. "I mean, I want to do it. But I planned on waiting until he was really ready before trying it with him again."

I look at Sneakers. His tail is wagging.

I look at Jane. Her face is glowing.

Maybe we should try. Maybe it'll do more than just cheer up the kids at the hospital.

Maybe it'll help cheer up Jane, too.

"Why not?" I answer back. "Let me call Gran."

TWELVE

I'm nervous when we get to the hospital. Maybe Sneakers isn't ready for this. What if he blows it again? What if I blow it? I guess my nervousness shows on my face.

Jane gives me a wink. "Don't worry. Sneakers will be fine. Just make sure you give him the firm, calm direction he needs."

But when we get to the children's ward, Nurse Bennett blocks our path. "Whoa, whoa, whoa," she says, holding up her hand. "Where do you think you're going?"

"We're here to visit the kids," Jane replies.

Nurse Bennett shakes her head. "Uh-uh. I don't think so, Jane. Not that dog. I remember what happened last time."

"Oh, that was the old days," Jane says, trying to soften her up. "Sneakers just had a bad day last time. Zoe has been training him all week, and he's doing just great. He's going to be a therapy dog. I'm sure the kids would love to see him."

Nurse Bennett puts her foot down. "Sorry, guys," she says. "But I'm afraid I have to say no."

"It's not fair," I say to Jane as we leave the hospital. "It's just not fair."

I feel awful. I feel as if it's all my fault. If I'd trained Sneakers better from the beginning, he wouldn't have misbehaved the last time we were at the hospital. We'd be inside right now, cheering up all those kids.

I put Sneakers down on the ground and hook his leash to his collar. I start to walk, staring at the ground.

"Don't worry, kiddo," Jane says, trying to console me as we walk back toward the car. "Temporary setback. We'll get you in sooner or later."

Suddenly the leash pulls tightly behind me. I look back.

Sneakers has stopped dead in his tracks and has started barking at something.

I'm not in the mood for this. "Come on, Sneakers." I tug on the leash.

Sneakers tugs back.

It's like he's misbehaving just to make me feel worse.

"Come, boy. Come!" I whistle, then clap my hands. "Come on, Sneak! Wanna go for a ride?"

But no matter what I say, he won't budge.

"Maybe the nurse is right," I tell Jane in frustration. "Maybe Sneakers just can't be trained. Maybe he just isn't cut out to be a therapy dog."

Sneakers barks again. Now he's tugging toward the side of the building.

"What's he barking at?" I ask Jane. I look up and all around. I don't see anything.

Sneakers tugs me across the grass toward a large window.

"What is it, boy?"

Sneakers stops in the grass and sits. He barks and barks at a large picture window.

Someone inside the hospital is looking out.

The sun glints off the window a moment, and I can't see who it is. Then Sneakers tugs me closer, and I can see.

It's Emma Morgan! She's sitting in her wheelchair, like always. I can't believe how different she looks from when I saw her over a week ago. She's thinner. Frailer. Slumped lower in her seat.

A ridiculous smiley-face balloon tied to her wheel-chair bobs above her head.

"Look, Jane," I say over my shoulder. "It's Emma."

Sneakers barks and barks.

Then I realize that Emma's not staring at nothing, like she usually does. She's looking at Sneakers.

Full of hope, I dash in front of Sneakers. "Come on, Sneakers. Let's show her what we can do!" I look him in the eye. I try to talk to him with all my thoughts, all my body language, all my heart. "Sit," I begin.

Sneakers sits like a prince! I want to scoop him up and swirl him around.

But instead, I try our hardest trick. "Come on, Sneak. Listen now. Roll over."

I make that rolling motion with my hand. I use all the ESP juice I can muster. "Roll over. Roll over, Sneak. You can do it! Roll over!"

Sneakers rolls over, then springs back onto his paws.

Ta-da! his little face seems to say.

"Wahoo!" I shout, jumping in the air. "Good boy!"

And then he does it again.

And again. I realize he's having fun!

I glance up at the window. And I see something even more wonderful.

Emma smiles.

More kids join Emma at the window now, trying to see what she's smiling at.

I wave at the kids—some that I know and some new ones. The kids smile and wave back. When they see Sneakers rolling around, they start to laugh and clap and tap on the window.

I scoop Sneakers up, and we both take a bow. Then I hold Sneakers up to the window. He tries to give Emma a kiss through the glass.

Emma blows him a kiss instead.

Then I see another face.

"Uh-oh." It's Nurse Bennett! She motions at me. I guess she's telling me to go away, to quit bothering the patients.

"What a party pooper!" I whisper to Sneakers. I hug him and turn away.

"Wait, Zoe." Jane puts a hand on my shoulder, stopping me. "Look."

I turn around. Nurse Bennett isn't scowling, like I expect her to be. She's shaking her head, but she's smiling! And waving at me.

"What?" I say, stepping forward.

I can't hear her, but I can read her lips.

"Come on in," she mouths. And she's waving at me to hurry.

"Really?" I exclaim.

She smiles and nods enthusiastically.

"I'll be right there!" I say. "Come on, Jane!"

We stop first so Sneakers can empty his tank. Then the three of us hurry inside.

Soon I'm sitting in the lounge, surrounded by kids. Sneakers rests quietly on Emma's lap as she strokes his fur. Stephanie is sitting on the floor beside them, trying to brush Sneakers' fur with a purple doll brush. For once Michael isn't cracking jokes, but he's got a new chew toy that he bought for Yum-Yum. He gives it to Sneakers instead.

That makes me feel great—to see that Sneakers isn't just mine. He's a dog that a lot of people can love.

It's funny. I started out doing this to help others. I never guessed how great it would make me feel.

What if I'd given up on Sneakers? What if I'd just quit trying to train him? We wouldn't be here now, cheering up these kids. Filling in for Yum-Yum.

I owe it to Jane, Gran, and even Maggie for helping me. I only wish Mom could see me now. She'd probably say, "This would make a great movie, Zoh!"

Standing back with Nurse Bennett, Jane looks happier than she's looked in a while. I hope helping me and Sneakers with our training will keep her busy as she learns to deal with losing Yum-Yum.

As soon as I get home, I'm going to call up that training program Jane told me about and find out how Sneakers and I can train in a real therapy dog program. Then Sneakers will be official!

I can't help but wonder as I watch everyone— what is it about a dog that makes people so happy? Especially kids like these, who have a whole lot to be unhappy about.

I don't know. Maybe it's because a dog just thinks about today. He doesn't worry about the future. He doesn't fret about the big messes he made yesterday! He's just trying to be happy *now*.

The kids have asked me to read a book, and I've found one that Emma's brother sent her. I open the cover to the title page. "Lassie Come Home," I read, then tell the kids, "This is Sneakers' favorite book. He *loves* stories that have a dog as the main character!"

Emma laughs. Her eyes shine. For the moment, all her problems are forgotten.

And then I begin to read.

I always love the beginning of a new story.

Pets On Call

By J.J. MACKENZIE, D.V.M.

WILD WORLD NEWS—Imagine being sick in a hospital, facing an operation, or undergoing cancer treatment. Or imagine having to move into a nursing home, perhaps far away from your home, family, and friends. The hours may seem to drag by. Pain may be a daily part of your life. You're bound to be a little lonely and sad.

Then someone comes to see you—someone who will sit with you, listen to you without judgment, make you laugh, and even love you—no questions asked.

And all that special someone wants in return is a pat on the head. That special someone is a dog! But not just any dog. He's an animal who has gone through many hours of special training so that he can go into the community to cheer up people in need of a little TLC—tender loving care.

Continued on page B10

Cloning Becomes a
Hot T

Continued from page B1

YOU HAVE A VISITOR

Every day around the country, thousands of dogs visit hospitals, schools, nursing homes, and rehabilitation centers. These trips range from quick, informal group visits to one-on-one sessions with  patients. Some highly trained pets even have gone into communities that have suffered from school violence or a natural disaster like a flood or an earthquake to help kids deal with their fears and learn to feel normal again.

People use a variety of terms to describe pets who visit people: "therapy pets," "therapy dogs," or "visiting pets." You may also hear their work referred to as "Animal Assisted Activities" (AAA) and "Animal Assisted Therapy" (AAT). AAA programs focus on visiting people to cheer them up and entertain them. In AAT, animals work directly with health-care workers like nurses and physical therapists to help patients recover from illnesses or disabilities.

A PET A DAY . . .

Dogs and other pets were once thought to be too dirty and unsanitary, or even too dangerous, to bring into health-care facilities. But those attitudes changed as studies began to show that interaction with pets can actually improve people's health.

Pet visits to a nursing home can help people feel less lonely and depressed and can improve their overall sense of well-being. A pet visiting a hospital can distract patients from their pain and help them feel more hopeful in dealing with medical treatment.

Research shows that just the act of petting a dog can lower blood pressure. Pets can also decrease feelings of isolation. And when pets visit regularly, it gives people something wonderful to look forward to.

Dogs have an amazing ability to break the ice between strangers and give them something to talk about. In fact, bringing a dog into an environment like a nursing home can encourage people to be more social, and the effect lasts even after the pet has gone.

HOW CAN MY DOG HELP?

Does AAA sound like something you and your pet might be interested in? Great—but don't rush off to your local hospital with Fido in tow! Both dogs and people need special training to make sure they're ready.

To begin with, your dog needs to be well trained. Can he reliably obey basic commands, such as "sit," "stay," "lie down," and "come"? Can he walk with you under your control or on a leash?

But it's not enough for your dog to be well trained. What's more important is whether he wants to do it. Take the quiz at the end of this article to find out.

GETTING STARTED

To learn more about how you and your pet can train to do AAA, check the library for books about pet therapy and read up on what to expect. Then look in your phone book for local organizations, or contact the nearest hospital or nursing home. Many health-care facilities will be involved with an established program and will be able to tell you where to get information. You can also search under "Pet Therapy" or "Animal Assisted Activities" online (ask a parent for permission and help).

Even people without pets can sign up to be part of a pet therapy program. Most programs are open to anyone age ten or older. Usually dogs must be at least one year old to participate.

Go to class. When you find an organization in your area, you'll be able to sign up for classes. You might study a handbook and watch videos of real pet visits. Many classes will even simulate situations that a dog might encounter on a real visit so that you and your dog can practice.

Get a check-up. Most organizations will require you to visit your veterinarian to make sure your pet is healthy, disease-free, and up-to-date on shots.

Pass the test. Many programs will require your dog to pass the American Kennel Club Canine Good Citizen Test. You can find out more about the test through the American Kennel Club or your local animal shelter or humane society.

Get to work. After you've completed training, the organization will evaluate your pet and certify that he's ready to go on visits. Once certified, you and your pet can make visits alone, with your family, or as part of a group. Many groups will even set up regular visits for you.

Just a pup? If your dog is less than one year old, you can still get started now. Practice basic obedience skills with your dog every day. Slowly help him get used to being around people outside of your family. Gradually practice taking him into crowds and unusual situations.

Payback. Training your pet to go into the community is a lot of hard work. But when you see the smiles on the faces of the people you and your dog visit, you'll know it's been worth every second.✦

IS YOUR PET A GOOD BET FOR THERAPY?

Circle yes or no.

1. Does my dog really like people?

   YES   NO

2. Does he stay calm when he walks through a crowd, meets a friendly stranger, or meets another dog?

   YES   NO

3. Is my dog comfortable being touched, hugged, and petted by people he doesn't know?

   YES   NO

4. Is he comfortable with loud voices and clumsy movements?

   YES   NO

5. Is he relaxed around moving equipment, such as wheelchairs or walkers?

   YES   NO   DON'T KNOW

If you answered YES to most of these questions, your pet may be a good candidate!

About the Author

Laurie Halse Anderson has had many pets—dogs, cats, mice, even salamanders. Her best dog was a German shepherd named Canute. She got him from a shelter when he was two years old. Canute was Laurie's constant running companion. He helped her get into shape for a half-marathon. A few summers ago, he died in her arms. She keeps his collar in her office for inspiration while writing.

Laurie has written many books for kids, including picture books and a young-adult novel. When she's not writing or teaching writing workshops at local schools, Laurie splits her time between bird-watching and hanging out at the local vet clinic. She lives in Ambler, Pennsylvania, with her husband, her two daughters, and a cat named Mittens.

Storm Rescue

Sunita
Vet Volunteer

Lucy looks awful. Her fur is matted from the rain. Her eyes are huge and scared. The lower part of her left front leg is swollen. Her mouth is open slightly, and she's panting sort of like a dog. That means she's in shock from the pain. She lets out a pitiful meow and tries to lift her head.

"What happened?" Dr. Mac asks as she carefully takes Lucy from Mrs. Clark.

"There was a big clap of thunder," Mrs. Clark says. "Lucy and I were both startled. She jumped out of my arms in a panic and hit the front door pretty hard."

I wince. Poor Lucy! But there's no time to think about that. Dr. Mac is already heading for the Herriot Room.

Maggie, David, and I follow her.

"Maggie, we need to anesthetize and X-ray.

David, get the splinting equipment ready in case there's a fracture. Sunita, watch her carefully for any signs of distress."

I nod and move quickly into place. "It's okay, sweetie," I croon to Lucy as soothingly as I can. I wish I could pet her to let her know everything will be okay, but I know I shouldn't. "Just stay still now."

Meanwhile Dr. Mac examines Lucy, gently but quickly checking her vital signs. She looks at the cat's gums. I see a flash of pale pink.

"She's in mild shock—not too bad," Dr. Mac says. "We'd better get a little oxygen into her and start her on some I.V. fluids. Then we'll put her under so I can take a closer look at her leg."

Dr. Mac puts an oxygen mask over Lucy's face. I hold it there while she inserts the I.V. catheter and starts the fluids. Then she moves away to help Maggie prepare the anesthetic.

"Hang in there, Lucy," I murmur, hoping she can feel the good thoughts I'm sending her.

Dr. Mac returns with a syringe. "Okay," she says. "This will make you feel better, girl." She injects the anesthetic with one smooth move.

I watch Lucy's eyelids droop lower and lower until she's unconscious.